WILLIAM CARRIES ON

"GOOD-BYE, MY DARLING," SAID THE LITTLE GIRL,
AS SHE THRUST THE RABBIT INTO WILLIAM'S ARMS.

(*See page* 212)

WILLIAM CARRIES ON

BY

RICHMAL CROMPTON

ILLUSTRATED BY

THOMAS HENRY

LONDON

GEORGE NEWNES LIMITED

TOWER HOUSE, SOUTHAMPTON STREET

STRAND, W.C. 2

First Published . . . May 1942
First Cheap Edition . . . November 1942

Printed in Great Britain by
Wyman & Sons, Limited, London, Fakenham and Reading.

CONTENTS

CHAPTER I

TOO MANY COOKS

"THERE'S some new people in Honeysuckle Cottage," said Ginger.

"There's always new people in Honeysuckle Cottage," retorted William.

The war had brought to the village a new and shifting population of evacuees, both official and unofficial. At first the Outlaws had been deeply interested in them, but by now they had become so much accustomed to them that they hardly noticed the changes. Few of the newcomers remained long. They either went on to stay with relatives still further out of the danger zone or, bored by the apparent lack of incident characteristic of English village life, returned to London.

But, as time elapsed, the new tenant of Honeysuckle Cottage began to interest the Outlaws deeply. She was a small vague rather shy woman who always seemed in a hurry and yet always seemed to have time for a little chat with them. She showed an interest in their concerns that was as unusual in a grown-up as it was flattering. She was interested in Red Indians and tracking and wood-craft and marbles and kites and trains and aeroplanes and bows and arrows and damming streams and climbing trees and making fires.

She invited the Outlaws to tea and regaled them with a meal of such pre-war deliciousness that they could hardly realise it was not a dream. It was then that she revealed the nature of the activities that occupied so much of her time.

"You see," she explained, "cookery's my job. I write about it in magazines, and I've had several books published on it. Of course," she sighed, "war-time cookery's a great problem, but," she brightened, "it's always fun to have a problem to tackle, isn't it?"

At tea they met her secretary, Miss Griffin, who was as small and vague and shy as her employer.

"Miss Griffin's business-like," said Mrs. Fountain in a tone of awe and admiration, "and she types beauti-fully. By the way, I'm going to try some war-time sweets to-morrow. If you'd like to come round after tea and sample them . . ."

The Outlaws assuredly would like to. They sampled them to the last crumb. Mrs. Fountain watched them anxiously.

"I do hope they're all right," she said with a question in her voice.

There was no question in the voices of the Outlaws as they assured her that they were most emphatically all right.

"That's very kind of you," she said gratefully.

"Then I'll get the recipes typed out to-night, shall I?" said Miss Griffin.

Mrs. Fountain took such an interest in the Outlaws' concerns that the Outlaws couldn't help taking an interest in hers. They knew the titles of the books she had written and the titles of the books she hoped to write; they knew the names of the magazines she contributed to and the names of the magazines she hoped to contribute to; they knew the recipes she had invented and the recipes she hoped to invent. . . . They had fallen into the habit of calling at Honeysuckle Cottage every day about tea-time and she always had some special delicacy, which she presented to them with the air of one asking. not conferring, a favour.

"I'm so glad you like it," she would say gratefully, and Miss Griffin, who always watched them as anxiously as her employer, would brighten and say: "I'll type out the recipe to-night, shall I?"

One afternoon the Outlaws arrived to find both Mrs. Fountain and her secretary in a state of suppressed excitement.

"He's coming to lunch on Tuesday," they said.

"Who?" demanded William.

"Mr. Devizes, the editor of *Woman's Mirror*," said Mrs. Fountain reverently. "I've been trying to get that Cookery Page for years. He says that he's coming to discuss the matter, but, of course, everything will depend on the lunch. Oh"—a far-away look came into her eyes—"how I wish I could get some lemons!"

"Can't you buy some?" asked William simply.

"My dear boy, there aren't any. Or, if there are, they're hidden."

"Hidden?"

Her small vague face took on an unaccustomed look of severity.

"Hoarded," she explained. "It's criminal, of course, and people can get put in prison for it, but they still do it. Oh, if only I had some lemons, I could cook a *marvellous* lunch!"

"What are you goin' to have for lunch?" asked William.

"Soup, first."

"You can't put lemons in soup, can you?" said William.

Mrs. Fountain sighed.

"I think I could if only I had them! But it's a lemon pudding I really want them for. I have a wonderful recipe for a lemon pudding. I think I'll have to make an apple pudding, but, of course, one really wants lemons even for that."

She seemed so preoccupied by the thought of the lunch, so harassed by the absence of lemons, that the Outlaws took their departure earlier than usual.

William walked home thoughtfully. Thoughtfully he entered the morning-room, where his mother sat darning socks.

"Mother," he began, "have you any——"

"For heaven's sake, William," said Mrs. Brown, "take that great stick out of the room. I'm sick and tired of picking up the sticks you leave all over the place. I can't think why you bring them in at all."

"What stick?" said William, surprised, then: "Oh, that!"

Whenever William went out, he secured a stick from wood or hedgerow in order to wave it about or slash at hedges with it or make lunges at imaginary enemies or use it as jumping pole or walking stick, according to its length. He did this so automatically and took the process so much as a matter of course that he was always genuinely surprised when the presence of these appendages was pointed out to him.

"Oh, that!" he said, looking down at the stout ash stick that he had laid down negligently across the settee.

"Take it into the hall if you must have it."

"Yes, I mus' have it," said William firmly. "It's a jolly fine stick."

He took it into the hall and returned to the morning-room.

"Mother," he began again, "have you any——"

Again Mrs. Brown interrupted him.

"Take your coat and muffler off if you've come home for tea, William."

"A'right," agreed William pacifically. "Mother, have you any——"

"*William!*" said Mrs. Brown. "Don't just throw them on to the floor. Take them into the hall and hang them on the hat-stand."

"Sorry," said William, gathering coat and muffler up from the floor. "I wasn't thinkin'. I've got a lot to think of jus' now."

He went into the hall, hung up his coat and muffler and returned to the morning-room. Seeing questions about face-washing and hair-brushing already trembling on his mother's lips, he said all in one breath:

"Motherhaveyougotanylemons?"

"*Lemons?*" said Mrs. Brown as if she could hardly believe her ears. "*Lemons?* I hardly remember what they look like."

"There's a picture of 'em in the 'cyclopædia," said William helpfully.

"I don't think I even want to remember what they look like," said Mrs. Brown bitterly. "No, I've not *seen* one for weeks."

B

"If you wanted to get hold of one," said William, "how would you start?"

"I shouldn't," said Mrs. Brown. "I've given it up. After all, it's no use breaking one's heart over a lemon."

"But suppose you *had* to have one," said William, "what would you do?"

"I shouldn't do anything," said Mrs. Brown. "What with onions and eggs and icing sugar and cream I've just given it up. There's nothing one *can* do."

"But suppose someone was dyin' an' wanted one," persisted William.

"I don't think they would," said Mrs. Brown, after giving due consideration to this question. "I mean, I can't imagine anyone wanting a lemon in those particular circumstances."

"I bet the thing would be to find one of those hoarders an' take 'em off him," said William.

"Now, William," said Mrs. Brown firmly, "stop talking nonsense about lemons and go and wash your face and brush your hair."

　　　　*　　　*　　　*　　　*　　　*

William walked slowly down the road towards the village. A night's sleep had brought him no nearer the solution of his problem. He was still determined to find a lemon or lemons for Mrs. Fountain, and he still believed that the best way of doing this would be to find a hoarder of lemons and rob him of some of his ill-gotten spoil, but the chief difficulty still remained. He couldn't find a hoarder of lemons. . . . He had mentioned lemons tentatively to several people and the wistfulness or bitterness—according to temperament—of their response had cleared them immediately of suspicion.

WILLIAM'S SCOWL DID NOT RELAX AS HIS EYES FELL
UPON VIOLET ELIZABETH.

"Lemons? Don't I wish I'd got one!"

Or: "Lemons? It's a shame, an outrage, a crying scandal. Hitler shall pay for this!"

He went to the village shop and demanded a lemon, only to be chased out of it by the indignant shopkeeper.

"Any more of your sauce an' I'll tell your Pa, you cheeky little nipper, you!"

"Bet I find one before I've finished," muttered William as he went on down the road. "Bet I do...."

It was just at this point that he ran into Violet Elizabeth Bott. Violet Elizabeth Bott was the daughter of the owner of the Hall—a gentleman of obscure origin who had made a fortune out of Bott's Digestive Sauce. She was seven years old and was possessed of considerable personal charm and a lisp. William was one of the few people who had never yielded to her charm, and she held him accordingly in respect and admiration.

"Hello, William," she greeted him with a flutter of her long eyelashes.

William's scowl did not relax as his eyes fell upon her.

"Hello," he replied distantly and was passing her by without stopping.

Violet Elizabeth, however, firmly barred his way with her small but solid person.

"Ith nith to thee you, William," she said, turning on the famous charm, but William was, as ever, proof against it.

"It's not nice to see you," he countered with regrettable discourtesy. "Get out of my way. I'm busy."

"I'm buthy, too," said Violet Elizabeth sweetly. "Leth be buthy together."

"*Gosh!*" said William severely. "D'you think I want *girls* meddlin' in my business?"

She smiled up at him delightedly. She was always thrilled by William's brusqueness.

"What ith your buthineth, William?" she coaxed.

William hesitated. His first instinct was to refuse to have any further dealings with this immature representative of a despised sex. Then he reconsidered his attitude. He must leave no stone unturned. A lemon hoarder might be discovered even in the most unlikely quarter.

"My business is lemons," he said curtly.

"Lemonth?" echoed Violet Elizabeth, opening her blue eyes wide in surprise. "Why lemonth, William?"

William looked at her.

"Have *you* got any lemons?" he said sternly.

She shook her golden curls.

"Me? No, William, I've not got any lemonth. Why thould I have any lemonth?"

"Dunno," said William morosely. "Dunno why anyone should have the beastly things. I wish they'd never been invented. I say, d'you know anyone that's got any?"

Violet Elizabeth considered, drawing her brows together in deep thought. Then she brightened.

"Yeth. Motherth got thome. Thee's got a whole bocth full. Thee'th had it in the bottom of her wardrobe for month an' month an' *month*."

"Corks!" said William, his eyes opening to their fullest extent. "She's a hoarder, then, that's what she is. A hoarder."

"Ith thee?" said Violet Elizabeth sweetly and without much interest.

"Yes, she is," said William sternly, "an' we've gotter get 'em off her. Gosh! She'll get put in prison, hoardin' all those lemons. You wouldn't like her to get put in prison, would you? I know someone what *needs* those lemons, so we've gotter get 'em from your mother, an' give 'em to this person what *needs* 'em."

"I'll athk her for them, thall I?" said Violet Elizabeth serenely.

"No, you'd better not do that," said William. "She wouldn't let you have 'em. She's a crim'nal— all hoarders are crim'nals—an' crim'nals get desp'rate when they're cornered."

"What thall I do, then?" asked Violet Elizabeth.

"Couldn't you get 'em without her knowin'?" asked William. "Well, I think you *ought* to stop her bein' a crim'nal an' gettin' put in prison. You wouldn't like her to get put in prison, would you?"

Violet Elizabeth considered the question.

"Yeth, I think I would," she said at last cheerfully. "I could thtay up ath late ath I like if thee wath in prithon. I've alwayth wanted to thtay up ath late ath I like."

"But you wouldn't get any pocket money," said William cunningly. He remembered Violet Elizabeth's greatest weakness. "You wouldn't be able to buy any acid drops."

Violet Elizabeth's face fell.

"Oh, don't let her be put in prithon, then, William," she pleaded. "I do tho love athid dropth."

"All right, I won't," said William with the air of a knight errant undertaking some dangerous and difficult task. "I'll try'n' do that for you. I'll try'n' stop your mother gettin' put in prison so's you can go on havin' acid drops. It's goin' to be jolly hard, but I'll do it jus' 'cause I don't want you not to have acid drops with your mother goin' to prison."

"Oh, *thank* you, William," said Violet Elizabeth gratefully. "You're *tho* kind."

"Well, the first thing to do," said William, so deeply impressed by his own cunning that for the moment he couldn't think what was the first thing to do. "Well—er—the first thing to do is to get those lemons off her before the police find out that she's got 'em an' start puttin' her in prison. Could you get 'em?"

"Oh, yeth, William," said Violet Elizabeth. "I could get them eathily. I know juth where they are. They've been there for month an' *month*."

"Well, you get 'em an' bring 'em along," said William. "Could you get 'em first thing to-morrow morning?"

"Oh, yeth," said Violet Elizabeth. She was silent for a moment then said: "I wouldn't mind her going to prithon for juth one day, William. I could do nearly all the thingth thee dothn't let me do in one day."

"Goodness!" said William. "They'd put her in prison for *years*. Jus' think. You'd have no acid drops for *years*. You wouldn't like that, would you?"

"Oo, no," agreed Violet Elizabeth with a shudder. "I thouldn't like that. I'll get the lemonth for you firtht thing to-morrow, then, William."

"All right," said William. "I'll be in your summerhouse d'rectly after breakfast an' you bring 'em along."

"Yeth, I will," promised Violet Elizabeth serenely.

True to her word, she came trotting along to the summer-house the next morning, carrying a cardboard box.

"Here they are, William," she said. "They're lovely lemonth. Thee needn't go to prithon now—need thee?—'cauth thee's going to take me to the pictureth an' I do tho want to go to the pictureth."

"No, it's all right now," William assured her. "She won't have to go to prison now."

"NO, IT'S ALL RIGHT NOW," WILLIAM ASSURED VIOLET
ELIZABETH.

He opened the box. There were six small lemons, each in a separate compartment.

"Thanks," he said gratefully. He took them out of the box and slipped them into the pocket of his coat, then hesitated.

"Seems sort of stealin' jus' to take 'em," he said, assailed suddenly and belatedly by faint scruples. "P'raps we oughter put some other sort of fruit in their place, then it'd only be exchangin'."

"What about appleth?" suggested Violet Elizabeth brightly. "We've got loth an' loth of appleth thtored in the bocth-room."

"Yes, that'll do fine," said William. "You fetch them an' we'll put 'em in, then it won't be stealin'."

Violet Elizabeth trotted off obediently, to return a few minutes later with six rosy apples.

"We'll put one in each hole, thall we?" she suggested. Then hopefully: "If thee openth it p'rapth thee'll forget it wath lemonth an' think it wath appleth all the time. Thee'th got a very bad memory. Thee'th alwath forgetting thingth."

At this moment a voice was heard from the direction of the house calling "Violet Eliza—*beth*!"

"P'rapth I'd better go," said Violet Elizabeth hurriedly. "They make thuth a futh if they think I'm lotht. You put the appleth into the holth, William, an' leave the bocth here an' I'll come back for it an' put it back where it wath in Mother'th cupboard."

"All right," agreed William.

He watched Violet Elizabeth trot off in the direction of the house, then turned his attention to the apples that she had put on the table. He fitted them slowly and carefully into the spaces of the box where the lemons had been. They were larger than the lemons and took up so much room that the lid didn't quite close. They were much too large for the box, thought William, looking at them longingly. . . . Perhaps if he just took one bite out of each they'd fit better and it wouldn't do any real harm. They'd look the same from the top anyway, and probably Mrs. Bott had forgotten all about the box by now, and would never think of it again. Violet Elizabeth had said that she had a very bad memory and the box had been there for months.

He took a bite out of the largest and most tempting-looking . . . then another . . . then another . . . then stood gazing down in horror at the core.

"Gosh!" he said aloud to himself in a tone of stern indignation. "Fancy eatin' it all! You'd better be more careful with the next."

He certainly meant to be more careful with the next. He meant to take only one—or at most two—bites out of it, but he happened to catch sight, through the summer-house window, of two sparrows fighting, and the spectacle so engrossed him that he found he had eaten the whole apple before he realised it. Again only the core was left. After that William surrendered to Fate. He was never a boy to go in for half measures. After all, one might as well eat six apples as two. He ate them with relish and dispatch and put the six cores carefully in the centres of the partitions in the box. They at least proved, he considered, his good intentions, were evidence that he had meant to replace the six lemons by six apples, and would have done so, had not Fate been too much for him. He shut the box, placed it on the seat of the summer-house, the precious lemons safely in his pocket, and quietly departed.

A few minutes after he had gone, Violet Elizabeth returned, took the box and put it back at the bottom of her mother's wardrobe.

She did not open the box, and therefore did not notice that it contained only six apple cores.

Neither she nor William had noticed that the lid of the box bore the words: "Lemon Soap. Guest Size."

*   *   *   *   *

No one seemed to be about when William approached Honeysuckle Cottage. Mrs. Fountain had given a lecture on war-time cookery to the Women's Institute yesterday afternoon, and Miss Griffin was busy typing out the notes of it. Mrs. Fountain herself had got the lunch under way and was upstairs changing her dress. William entered the cottage by the back door and looked about the kitchen uncertainly. It would be nice, he thought, if the lemons could come as a surprise, if Mrs. Fountain, thinking that she had no lemons for lunch, could suddenly and unexpectedly find that she had. A saucepan was boiling on the gas stove. William lifted the lid and sniffed tentatively. Soup. Unmistakably soup. He remembered Mrs. Fountain's saying that she would put lemons into soup if she had them, so he slipped two of the lemons from his pocket into the soup. She should have lemons in her soup and it should come as a lovely surprise. . . .

Then he opened the oven door, Some sort of meat was cooking in a casserole. You couldn't have lemons in meat. It was a pity but there it was. . . . On another shelf of the oven some sort of pudding was cooking. William remembered that Mrs. Fountain had said that she was going to have an apple pudding and that you needed lemons for apple pudding. There was a sort of crust on the top. Very carefully he moved the crust aside and slipped a lemon underneath, replacing the crust so that no one would know it had been disturbed. Another lovely surprise for her, he thought with satisfaction. He still had three more lemons, but he didn't see how he could use them. He'd put them on the larder shelf, so that she could have a lemon pudding to-morrow. . . .

*   *   *   *   *

Mr. Devizes arrived at Honeysuckle Cottage on the stroke of one o'clock. He had had a long and troublesome journey and he was looking forward to a good lunch. He had thought that he would enjoy a day in the country, but the country had proved disappointing. It was definitely unlike the country that his pre-war memories and the views depicted on the cards and calendars he had received at Christmas had led him to expect. The trees dripped in a drizzle of rain, and the horizon was shrouded in a grey mist. It made him look forward to his lunch all the more. Some of Mrs. Fountain's recipes—even the war-time ones—had made his mouth water. He had the contract for the Cookery Page in his attaché case all ready for her signature.

Ah, this must be the cottage. A nice neat little cottage with a nice neat little garden. It suggested homeliness and comfort and—good food. A small boy seemed to be skulking in the bushes outside one of the windows. A gardener's boy, probably, intent on acquiring a gardener's skill in appearing to be engaged in some horticultural pursuit while in reality doing nothing at all.

He knocked at the door. A small woman with grey hair and a pleasant expression opened the door.

"Mrs. Fountain?" said Mr. Devizes.

"No. I'm her secretary, Miss Griffin. Do come in. . . ."

Mrs. Fountain was in the sitting-room hovering about a bottle of sherry. He liked the sherry and he liked Mrs. Fountain and he liked Miss Griffin and he liked the cottage and he was sure that he was going to like the lunch.

Mrs. Fountain led him into the pleasant little dining-room with yellow curtains and table mats, and a bowl of bronze chrysanthemums in the middle of the table.

"Now I'm going to ask you to excuse me while you have your soup," said Mrs. Fountain. "I'm not taking soup and I have one or two finishing touches to put to the rest of the meal."

She set down two steaming soup bowls on the table and scurried back to the kitchen.

William, from the shelter of the bushes outside the window, watched with interest. Now he would see the result of the trouble he had taken to make this meal a success. He waited confidently for smiles of delight and surprise to appear on the faces of the lunchers . . . but he waited in vain.

Mr. Devizes tasted his soup, and a peculiar expression spread over his countenance. It certainly contained surprise, but there was no delight in it. He laid down his spoon with an air of finality.

"So sorry," he said. "I ought to have told you that I didn't take soup. I'm afraid that I wasn't listening to what Mrs. Fountain said. I—I never take soup."

Miss Griffin murmured perfunctory sympathy. She

was obviously wrestling with some deep emotion. She took another spoonful . . . and another . . . and another. . . . Priscilla had evidently tried some new flavouring in the soup, and it wasn't a success. At least one couldn't say that anything of dear Priscilla's wasn't a success, but, whatever it was, it was an acquired taste . . . and it didn't seem easy to acquire. On the contrary it seemed extremely difficult. She'd already drunk more than half her bowl and it tasted as queer as ever. It was making her feel queer, too. . . . But one couldn't let dear Priscilla down. One must just go on. . . . She went on determinedly, her small face a mask of anguish. Mr. Devizes watched her with mingled horror and admiration. How on earth could she eat the stuff? But probably she was used to it. Probably they lived on these foul concoctions. He was glad that a merciful Providence had prevented his giving Mrs. Fountain the contract to sign before lunch. He couldn't possibly give his precious Cookery Page to a woman who turned out stuff like this.

Mrs. Fountain had come back into the room. "I do hope you liked the soup. . . . Oh, dear!" Her face fell as she looked at Mr. Devizes' bowl. "Oh, dear! You've hardly eaten any."

"I—I don't take soup," said Mr. Devizes. "I'm afraid I forgot to mention it in time."

"I hope it was all right," said Mrs. Fountain anxiously to Miss Griffin.

"It was lovely," said Miss Griffin, her lips set in a mirthless smile. (One mustn't let dear Priscilla down.) "It was simply delicious."

Mrs. Fountain looked at her in surprise. There was something almost hysterical in dear Lavinia's voice, and—how odd she looked! Perhaps she was finding the strain too much. It was, of course, a very important occasion. But there was nothing for her to worry about. She threw her a reassuring smile.

"I'll get in the meat, then," she said. "No, don't move. I like to be waitress. I know just where everything is."

Miss Griffin stood up as if to assist, then sat down suddenly, staring glassily in front of her.

A pity Mr. Devizes didn't like soup, thought William regretfully, as he watched Mrs. Fountain collecting the soup bowls and bustling out of the room. He'd missed a jolly good taste of lemon. The meat would be a bit dull, of course, because there wasn't any lemon in it, but there was a good bit of lemon in the pudding. It would be a jolly nice surprise for all of them to find the lemon in the pudding. Mr. Devizes would probably give Mrs. Fountain twice as much money as he'd meant to for the Cookery Page once he'd tasted the pudding. . . .

Mr. Devizes' spirits rose when he tasted the veal stew. It was delicious and quite definitely pre-war. There were peas in it and—yes, actually onions—and bacon and little balls of forcemeat and a delicious flavour of herbs. It was succulent and savoury and—in short, delicious. Yes, she certainly could cook. Perhaps he hadn't given the soup a fair trial. After all, he'd only had one spoonful. . . .

Miss Griffin ate her veal stew slowly, and didn't take much part in the conversation. That new soup of Priscilla's had left the oddest taste in her mouth. It made even this delicious veal stew taste queer. A most extraordinary taste. . . . Not really pleasant at all.

Mrs. Fountain changed the plates and brought in the pudding and a wine jelly. Mr. Devizes and Miss Griffin chose the pudding, Mrs. Fountain the jelly. Miss Griffin served the pudding, and her heart sank afresh as she did so. It was of a most curious consistency. Oh dear! Priscilla must have been trying another experiment, and it hadn't come off. So unlike dear Priscilla . . . and so unlike dear Priscilla's experiments. She took a mouthful and blenched. It surely couldn't taste as bad as that. Perhaps it was the taste of the soup that was still haunting her. Perhaps, she thought wildly, she was ill, and this dreadful taste was one of the symptoms. Yes, that must be it. Nothing —certainly nothing that dear Priscilla had cooked— could possibly taste as horrible as the soup had seemed to taste and as the pudding now seemed to taste. She must be ill. . . . As a matter of fact she felt ill. Very ill indeed. But one mustn't let dear Priscilla down.

"Delicious!" she murmured faintly as she carried yet another spoonful to her lips with a nerveless hand.

Mr. Devizes took a spoonful . . . and the smile froze on his lips. He'd never tasted anything so foul in all his life. Still, he'd give it a fair trial. He took three spoonfuls and each was fouler than the last.

Mrs. Fountain ate her wine jelly slowly and contentedly at the head of the table. The bowl of chrysanthemums hid both Mr. Devizes' and Miss Griffin's plates from her. She prattled away gaily about the weather and the garden and the village and the war.

"I don't see how they can get far if they do invade," she said. "There are tank traps all the way along Hadley High Street."

Miss Griffin rose abruptly from her seat. She had

drained the bitter cup to its dregs and a pea-green world rocked about her.

"I don't feel very well, Priscilla," she managed to articulate. "I—I think I'll go and rest."

With that she plunged from the room.

Mrs. Fountain gazed after her in surprise. Poor Lavinia! She certainly looked pretty bad. Such a pity that she was taken ill to-day of all days, when there was such a delicious lunch!

She craned her head round the chrysanthemums to see if Mr. Devizes had finished his pudding. He had evidently only had a few mouthfuls, but he had put his fork and spoon together.

"I'm sorry," he said. "I—I ought to have told you. I—I never take sweets."

"Oh, dear!" said Mrs. Fountain, disappointed. "What a pity! It's a speciality of my own. Don't you like it?"

"Delicious," said Mr. Devizes faintly. "But, as I said, I never touch sweets. I'm—er—inclined to be liverish."

Yes, he didn't look any too good, thought Mrs. Fountain, inspecting him critically. The weather, perhaps. It frequently upset the digestion.

"I really don't think that it could have done you any harm," she said wistfully. "But you must let me give you the recipe," she went on. "It's really delicious."

"Er—thank you," murmured Mr. Devizes.

He had decided—reluctantly but quite firmly—not to hand over his Cookery Page to her. The stew, of course, had been all right, but the soup and the sweet had been ghastly. The very memory of them made

c

him feel sick. Again he thanked his stars that he hadn't asked her to sign the contract before lunch. He'd nearly done so. She'd have killed off his readers like flies.

"'Fraid I must run away now," he said uncomfortably.

"Oh, but won't you have coffee?" pleaded Mrs. Fountain.

"I—I never take coffee," he said firmly. (Heaven alone knew what her coffee would be like!)

"B-but," she faltered, "I thought—I'd hoped that we were going to have a little business talk."

"I'll write," he said uncomfortably. "I'll write. Thank you so much for your hospitality."

She gazed at him in dismay. She knew as well as if he had told her in so many words that he'd changed his mind about the Cookery Page, that he wasn't going to give it to her, after all. It was so dreadful that she could hardly believe it.

"B-b-but," she began and was aghast to find herself on the verge of tears.

"Good-bye," he said hurriedly. "'Fraid I must fly. Got an important engagement in Town. . . ."

He dived towards the door and—ran into Mrs. Bott and Violet Elizabeth.

Mrs. Bott carried a box tied up in brown paper. She was impressively dressed in her visiting clothes, and seemed to fill the little room so completely that she left no means of escape. Mr. Devizes stared at her, fascinated by her bulk and the magnificence of her ospreyed hat and fur-trimmed coat.

Mrs. Fountain, still aghast and bewildered by the dashing of her most treasured hopes, introduced them.

"Pleased to meet you, I'm shar," said Mrs. Bott affably. She turned to Mrs. Fountain. "We all enjoyed your little talk so much at the W.I. yesterday, Mrs. Fountain, and we thought that we'd like to make you a little acknowledgment. Just a teeny trifle to mark our appreciation, as it were. Nothing much, of course, but war's war, so to speak, and we all 'ave to draw in our 'orns these days. It's just a little something to show you 'ow much we appreciated your kindness."

She handed the box to Mrs. Fountain with the air of Royalty presenting some coveted decoration, and stood smiling complacently as Mrs. Fountain unwrapped it. Mrs. Fountain laid the brown paper neatly aside and opened the box, revealing six compartments, in the middle of each of which reposed an apple core. This insult, coming on top of her recent disappointment, was too much for her. She dropped on to the settee and burst into tears. Violet Elizabeth, who had been unaware that the box her mother had brought with her was the one that had lain for so long in her wardrobe, and who had been watching proceedings with an air of boredom, started in sudden surprise.

"It muth be William," she said indignantly. "He'th eaten them. The greedy boy!"

"Eaten them?" said Mrs. Bott, who was staring at the apple cores in amazement. "Eaten what?"

"The appleth," said Violet Elizabeth.

"Apples!" screamed Mrs. Bott, succumbing into the settee next the weeping cookery expert. "*What* apples?"

"There were thix of them," said Violet Elizabeth. "Thix lovely appleth an' he'th eaten them all. He'th

"EATEN THEM?" SAID MRS. BOTT WHO WAS STARING
AT THE APPLE CORES IN AMAZEMENT. "EATEN
WHAT?"

a *greedy* boy. If I'd known he wath going to eat them
I'd have had thome too."

"I don't know what the child's talking about," said
Mrs. Bott helplessly to the others. "It was a box of
soap."

"THE APPLETH," SAID VIOLET ELIZABETH.

Violet Elizabeth shook her head.

"There wathn't ever any thoap in it," she said firmly.

"It was beautiful pre-war soap," wailed Mrs. Bott. "It had been left over from our last sale, but it was *good* soap, and I thought it would make a nice little gift."

"It wath appleth," said Violet Elizabeth with quiet persistence.

"It was *not* apples, you bad untruthful child!" said Mrs. Bott hysterically. "D'you think I don't know what's apples and what isn't? I tell you it was soap."

"Oh, no," agreed Violet Elizabeth, carrying her mind with difficulty back into the past. "It wathn't alwath appleth. It wath lemònth firtht."

"Lemons?" said Mrs. Bott, who had quite forgotten the particular kind of soap the box had contained. "I never heard such a thing! Am I mad or are you?"

"I'm not," said Violet Elizabeth reassuringly. "An' it *wath* lemonth. It wath lemonth firtht an' then it wath appleth, 'cauth of you goin' to prithon."

"*What!*" gasped Mrs. Bott. "*Me* goin' to *prison*?"

"Yeth," said Violet Elizabeth, unperturbed. "You were goin' to be put in prithon for hoardin' thingth an' William wanted to thave you 'cauth of athid dropth an' you taking me to the pictureth, tho he took out the lemonth and put appleth in inthtead but he'th a *greedy* boy."

"Stop!" said Mrs. Bott, her usually resonant voice a mere whisper. "The child's mad. Stark, staring——"

"Wait a minute," said Mr. Devizes, picking up the cardboard box from the floor. "Perhaps this will explain it. 'Lemon Soap. Guest Size.'"

"Oh, I didn't know it wath thoap," said Violet Elizabeth. "William didn't know it wath thoap either." She started suddenly and pointed to the window. "He'th there. He'th lithening."

William, aware that events had taken a dramatic

turn but unable to hear what was being said, had inadvertently thrust his head right through the open window. At Violet Elizabeth's cry of discovery he dived back into the bushes, but too late. Mr. Devizes reached out of the window and grabbed him by the ear.

"Lemme go," said William, wriggling helplessly in his grasp. "Lemme go. . . . All right, I won't run away if you'll lemme go."

"Tell us the whole story," said Mr. Devizes sternly.

"All right," said William, standing at the open window and nursing his ear, which Mr. Devizes had now released. "It wasn't my fault. Honest, it wasn't my fault. I knew she wanted to give you a good lunch 'cause of this cookery page an' she wanted some lemons an' she hadn't any an' Violet Elizabeth said there were some in a box in her mother's bedroom an' I told her it was hoardin' an' she'd get put in prison an' she said she'd get 'em an' she did an' I brought 'em here an' I wanted 'em to be a surprise an' I went into the kitchen when no one was there an' I put two in the soup an' one in the puddin' 'cause I wanted her to get this cookery page an' I put the rest in the larder." He paused a moment for breath then continued. "You see I di'n't know that he di'n't like soup or puddin' an' that Miss Griffin wasn't feelin' well or I wouldn't've wasted 'em like that. . . ."

Mr. Devizes burst into a roar of laughter.

"So *that's* what it tasted of," he said. "Lemon soap. Guest size."

"Oh, *dear*!" said Mrs. Fountain, aghast. "No wonder you didn't take soup or pudding."

It was at this point that Miss Griffin entered the room again. She looked pale and wan but mistress of herself.

"I'm so sorry," she apologised. "I don't know what came over me."

"We do," said Mr. Devizes. "It was 'Lemon Soap. Guest size'." He held out his hand and solemnly shook hands with her. "Allow me to congratulate you. You behaved like a heroine. You ate it to the last sud."

William had now entered the room by the door in order to justify himself more fully.

"*She*," nodding to Violet Elizabeth, "said they were lemons, and *she*," nodding to Mrs. Fountain, "said she *wanted* lemons. How was I to know it was soap?"

"Fanthy eating them all!" said Violet Elizabeth. "He ith a *greedy* boy!"

"'Ere! I still don't know what's 'appened," said Mrs. Bott, dropping aitches wildly in her bewilderment. "'Ow could the boy eat a boxful of soap and leave apple cores?"

"Let's all have some coffee," said Mrs. Fountain. "I'm sure we need it. You'll have some now, won't you?" to Mr. Devizes.

"Yes, please," he replied. "I'll have some with pleasure now that I know there won't be any lemon soap in it. . . . Let me give you a hand with it. Miss Griffin ought to sit still and rest. She's been through a very trying experience."

"Well," admitted Miss Griffin, smiling faintly, "I do feel a tiny bit *shaky* still."

Mrs. Fountain and Mr. Devizes went into the kitchen and returned soon afterwards with the coffee. Mrs. Fountain's small good-humoured face was alight with pleasure.

"We've fixed up the contract for the Cookery Page,"

she said to Miss Griffin. "I've signed it on the kitchen table. And he says he can get me some broadcasting. Isn't it wonderful!"

"I do wish I knew what's 'appened," said Mrs. Bott plaintively as she took her cup of coffee. "Lemons an' soap an' apple cores an' cookery pages! It's all beyond me." She sipped her coffee and her face brightened. "This 'ere's the best coffee I've 'ad since war started. 'Ow d'you make it?"

"Mrs. Fountain is probably going to broadcast on the making of coffee," said Mr. Devizes.

"Lawks!" said Mrs. Bott, impressed.

William sat sunk in deep dejection.

"I thought I was helpin' to make it a jolly good lunch," he said. "How was I to know it was soap?"

"Cheer up, old chap," said Mr. Devizes. "You've given me my first good laugh since the blitz started. I think that's worth half a crown."

"Gosh!" said William brightening. "Half a *crown!* Coo! *Thanks!*"

"Well, I give them apple cores up," sighed Mrs. Bott, "but it's such lovely coffee that I don't care *what* 'appened."

"I think I will try some coffee, dear," said Miss Griffin. "I'm feeling better every minute."

"I can tell the girlth at thchool that I know thome-one that broadcathts," said Violet Elizabeth proudly.

"I've always wanted to broadcast," said Mrs. Fountain.

"Coo!" murmured William ecstatically. "Half a crown! I'd almost forgot what they look like."

"Oh, it's not a bad old war at times," said Mr. Devizes, summing up the situation.

CHAPTER II

WILLIAM AND THE BOMB

IT caused quite a sensation among the Outlaws when they heard that the Parfitts were coming back from London to live in the village again because of the war. Joan Parfitt was the only girl of whom the Outlaws had ever really approved. She was small and dark and shy and eager and considered the Outlaws the embodiments of every manly virtue. They were afraid that her sojourn in London might have spoilt her, but to their relief they found that she had not altered at all. She was still small and dark and shy and eager, and she still considered the Outlaws the embodiments of every manly virtue. She was not even infected by the bomb snobbery that the inhabitants of the village found so exasperating in most of its London visitors. She did not describe her methods of dealing with "incendiaries," her reactions to "screamers," her shelter life, the acrobatics she performed when taking cover at various sinister sounds.

The village was sick of such descriptions from evacuees. It was perhaps unduly sensitive on the subject, suffering from what might be called a bomb inferiority complex. For, though enemy aeroplanes frequently roared overhead during the night watches, and a neighbouring A.A gun occasionally made answer, providing the youthful population with the shrapnel necessary for their "collections," no bombs had as yet fallen on the village.

Mrs. Parfitt had taken Lilac Cottage, recently vacated by Miss Cliff, and there the Outlaws went to call for Joan the morning after her arrival.

"It's lovely to be back," she greeted them. "I can hardly believe it's true."

The Outlaws were flattered by this attitude.

"I expect London's a bit more excitin' really," said William modestly.

"London's *horrible*," said Joan with a shudder. "All streets and houses. I can't *tell* you how horrible it is."

"Well, come on," said William happily. "Let's go to the woods an' play Red Indians."

For in the old days Joan had always been their squaw, and no one else had ever been found to fill the rôle satisfactorily.

In the course of the morning, during which Joan showed no falling off in her squaw performance, it turned out that she would celebrate her birthday while she was staying in the village.

"And Mummy says I can have a birthday party," she said. "It would have been terribly dull in London, but it will be lovely to be able to have you all to a birthday party."

Further investigation revealed that Joan's birthday was on the same day as Hubert Lane's. And then the Outlaws became really excited. For Hubert Lane— the inveterate enemy of the Outlaws—was having a birthday of (as far as possible) pre-war magnificence and he was inviting to it all his own supporters. He had, indeed, arranged the party chiefly in order to exclude from it the Outlaws and their friends and to jeer at them as the Boys who were not Going to a Birthday Party. He was aghast when he heard about Joan's. He continued to jeer, but a note of anxiety crept into his jeering.

"We're goin' to have jellies," he shouted to the Outlaws, when he met them in the village.

"So're we," the Outlaws shouted back.

"We're goin' to have a trifle."

"So're we."

".We're goin' to have crackers."

"So're we."

Joan's mother appreciated the importance of the occasion. Without aspiring to put Hubert's in the shade, the Outlaws' party (for so they looked on it) was to be every bit as good.

"We're goin' to get Mr. Leicester to come an' bring his kinematograph," said Hubert.

"He won't," said William. "He's a warden an' he says he's not got time. We've tried him."

"Then we'll borrow it off him. My mother can work it."

"So can Joan's mother, but he won't lend it. We've tried."

"Huh!" said Hubert. "I bet he'll lend it *us*."

But he was wrong. Mr. Leicester most emphatically refused either to bring his kinematograph to the party or to lend it.

In pre-war days the crowning glory of every children's party for miles round had been Mr. Leicester's kinematograph. It was his greatest pride and joy, and he loved to take it about with him and show it off. No children's party indeed was complete without Mr. Leicester, his kinematograph and his collection of Mickey Mouse films. No date was ever fixed for a party without first making sure that Mr. Leicester would be free. . . .

Since the war, however, Mr. Leicester had become a District Warden and was taking life very seriously. He had no time for such childish things as kinematographs and had, in fact, locked it up in the big cupboard in his dressing-room, announcing that it would not reappear till after the war. He refused indignantly all suggestions that he should lend it. No one but he, he said, understood its delicate mechanism.

Approached by the organisers of both parties, Mr. Leicester remained firm. Did they realise, he asked sternly, that there was a war on and that such things as kinematographs were wholly out of place? He would neither bring it nor lend it. It should not, in fact, see the light of day till Victory should have crowned the wardens' efforts (for Mr. Leicester considered the war to be waged entirely by wardens, magnificently ignoring army, navy and air force). Then, and not till then, he would take it out, and it would accompany him on the usual round of local festivities. . . .

Both the Outlaws and the Hubert Laneites finally resigned themselves to the absence of this central attraction, but rivalry between them still ran high.

"We're goin' to have some jolly excitin' games."

"So're we."

"We're goin' to have some you've never heard of."

"An' we're goin' to have some *you've* never heard of."

"Anyway, you're not goin' to have Mr. Leicester's cinema thing."

"Neither are *you*."

Hubert was afraid that the Outlaws, being admittedly more enterprising than his own followers, would evolve a more exciting programme for Joan's party than he and his followers could evolve for theirs.

"Wish somethin'd *happen* to them," he muttered darkly as he passed Lilac Cottage and saw through the window Joan and her mother making decorations for the party out of some coloured paper left over from Christmas.

And—as if his wishes had the power of a magician's wand—something *did* happen.

The bomb fell that night.

It was literally a bomb.

For the first time since the outbreak of war a German bomber, passing over the village, chose, for no conceivable reason, to release part of its load there.

Fortunately, most of it fell in open country and there were no casualties, but one bomb fell in the roadway just outside the Hall, blew up the entrance gates and made a deep crater in the road.

Mr. Leicester, complete with overalls and tin hat, was on the spot immediately. It was he who descried, at the bottom of the crater, the smooth rounded surface of a half-buried "unexploded bomb."

All through the months of inactivity he had longed for an Occasion to which he could rise, and he rose to this one superbly. The road must be roped off. Traffic must be diverted. All houses in the immediate neighbourhood must be evacuated. Fortunately the

Botts were away, so the many complications that Mrs. Bott would inevitably have introduced into the situation were absent. But Lilac Cottage was among the houses that Mr. Leicester ordered to be evacuated, and at first Mrs. Parfitt did not know where to go. Then Miss Milton came to the rescue. Miss Milton was prim and elderly and very very house-proud. She had had several evacuees billeted on her, but none of them had been able to stay the course and all had departed after a few weeks. So now she had a spare bedroom to offer Mrs. Parfitt and Joan.

"I shall look on it as my war work," she said to Mrs. Parfitt. "It will mean a good deal of inconvenience for me—I quite realise that—but one must put up with inconvenience these days."

Mrs. Parfitt hesitated.

"It's *very* kind of you," she said at last. "I hope, of course, that it won't be for long. Poor Joan! We were going to have her birthday party at the end of the month."

Miss Milton paled.

"A *party*!" she gasped. "She must not, of course, expect anything of that sort in *my* house. I was going to make it a condition that no other child entered the house at all. I have a *horror* of children, and I shall expect Joan to conform to the rules I laid down for my other evacuees. . . . You will be coming at once, I suppose?"

Mrs. Parfitt sighed.

"Yes. . . . Thank you so much. I hope we shan't trouble you for long."

But days passed and still the bomb failed to explode. The spirits of the Hubert Laneites rose.

"*Yah!*" they jeered. "Who's not goin' to have a birthday party?"

They taunted Joan and the Outlaws with the dainties they were preparing for their own feast, following them through the village and shouting:

"Trifle . . . jellies . . . choc'late cake. . . . An' *who's* not goin' to have any of 'em? *Yah!* Who's not goin' to have a party at all? *Yah!*"

It seemed, indeed, very unlikely that Joan's party would take place now. Mr. Leicester would go at frequent intervals to lean over the barrier and gaze with fond but modest pride at his unexploded bomb.

"No," he would say, "I don't know when it will go off. It might go off any minute or it might not go off for weeks. I am taking every precaution."

Meantime Joan was not finding life easy at Miss Milton's. Miss Milton had drawn up an elaborate code of rules. Joan was not to use the front door. She was to take off outdoor shoes immediately on entering the house. She was not to speak at meals. If inadvertently she touched any article of furniture, Miss Milton would leap at it with a duster, lips tightly compressed, in order to rub off any possible finger marks. Miss Milton rested upstairs in her bedroom from lunch time till tea time. She was, she said, a "light sleeper," so Joan had to creep about the house during that time on tiptoe and not raise her voice above a whisper.

After a week of this both Joan and her mother began to look pale and worn, but it was not till the afternoon before the date of what was to have been her birthday party that Joan finally gave up hope.

"YOU LEAVE IT TO ME," SAID WILLIAM BETWEEN HIS
TEETH. "I'LL FIX IT . . ."

William found her sobbing at the bottom of Miss
Milton's garden.

"I've been trying not to cry so as not to worry
Mummy," she sobbed, "but I can't help it. Oh,
William, it's horrible. I was looking forward to the
party so much and it would have been to-morrow and

D

I can't bear it. . . . It's so hateful here and Miss Milton's always cross and Hubert Lane shouts out after me about the party whenever I go out and . . . Oh, I'm so miserable I don't know what to do."

William considered the situation. He, too, had been pursued down the road from a safe distance by the jeers of the Hubert Laneites. Things seemed pretty hopeless. . . .

"And they'll be worse still afterwards," said Joan. "They'll never let us forget it. I did so want to have the party to-morrow. Oh, William," she fixed brimming eyes on him beseechingly, "can't you *do* something about it?"

The appeal went to William's head. He could not meet those tear-filled eyes and admit that he was powerless to help. He was not in any case a boy who liked to own himself at a loss. . . .

He assumed an expression of dare-devil recklessness and set his cap at a gangster-like angle.

"You leave it to me," he said between his teeth. "I'll fix it. . . ."

The tear-filled eyes widened. Hope shone through despair.

"Oh, William, *can* you?"

He gave a short laugh.

"Can I?" he repeated. "Huh! *Can* I? There's not many things I can't do, let me tell you!"

"Oh, *William* but . . ." Her face clouded again. "To-morrow? . . . It's so near."

"Huh!" he snorted contemptuously. "To-morrow's nothin' to me, to-morrow isn't."

Her small expressive face shone once more with hope and admiration.

"Oh William, you are wonderful!"

"'Course I'll fix it up by to-morrow," he said. "Now jus' don't you worry about it any more. You jus' leave it all to me. I'll get it all fixed up for you by to-morrow easy. You'll have your party an'—an'"—he lost his head still further—"Mr. Leicester'll bring his cinema thing an' it'll all be all right."

One—comparatively sane—part of him seemed to raise its voice in protest as it heard these more than rash promises, but William turned a deaf ear to it.

"Everythin'll be all right," he went on loudly as if to shout down the unseen opponent. "You jus' leave it all to me."

"An' we can go home to-morrow?" said Joan.

"'Course you can," said William.

Joan drew a deep sigh, smiling blissfully through her tears.

"Oh William!" she said. "You are wonderful. *Thank* you!"

"Quite all right," said William airily, though there was something fixed and glassy in the smile that answered hers. "Well, I'd better be gettin' off to see about it."

He swaggered out of the garden gate and set off down the road. As soon as he reached the bend that hid him from Joan's sight his swagger dropped from him and he began to argue fiercely as if with the still small voice of sanity. . . . "Well, why shouldn't I? . . . Well, I bet I can. . . . Well, I couldn't let her go on cryin' like that . . . I bet I can find a way all right . . . I bet I can . . . I bet I can fix it up. . . . Well," impatiently, "I've gotter *think*, haven't I? Gimme time to think . . . I bet I can think of a way. I——"

He stood still in the middle of the road staring in front of him, and the grim expression of his face gave place to one of rapture.

Quite suddenly he had thought of a way. It was so simple that he couldn't imagine why he hadn't thought of it before.

All he had to do was to move the unexploded bomb from the front of Joan's house to the front of Hubert Lane's house. Then Joan would be able to have her party, and Hubert Lane would not be able to have his. There was an element of poetic justice in the idea that appealed to him strongly. Joan would be able to have her party and Hubert Lane would not be able to have his. . . . Even the details of the plan did not seem difficult. He must, of course, wait till no one was about. . . . The bomb was not as closely guarded as it had been at the beginning. Even the policeman, whose duty it had been to stand by the barrier, was now generally away on other duties. There was very little traffic on that road in any case, and the inhabitants, once passionately interested in the bomb, had become bored by it and looked on it merely as a nuisance. Occasionally Mr. Leicester still came to gaze at it tenderly over the barrier, his eyes gleaming with the pride of possession. His bomb, his beloved unexploded bomb. . . . It justified, he felt, his whole career as a warden, gave his life meaning and purpose and inspiration. . . .

William realised, of course, that the thing might go off as he was removing it to Hubert Lane's house, but he considered himself quite capable of dealing with that. A saucepan on his head, a tin tray in readiness to use as a shield . . . and then, he thought, the bomb might do its worst. It was too large for him to carry, so he decided to take his ancient and battered soap box on wheels, which was his ordinary means of conveyance and which served regularly the purposes of train, motor car, highwayman's horse or pirate ship as needed in the Outlaws' games. . . . He would wait till the coast was clear, make his way down the crater, lift the unexploded bomb into the wooden cart, trundle it down the road to the Lanes' house and leave it there. The policeman or Mr. Leicester would soon find it, evacuate the Lanes, bring Joan and her mother back from Miss Milton's and—all would be well. Hubert would not be able to have his party and Joan would be able to have hers. . . .

He waited till dusk, put saucepan, tray and spade into his wooden cart and wheeled it off down the road to the barrier outside what had been the Hall gates. The road was empty. The crater lay invitingly easy of access in front of him, with the "unexploded bomb" in the centre. He glanced around, put the saucepan on his head, slipped under the barrier and climbed down into the crater. He dug carefully all round the bomb. It was bigger than he had thought it would be. It was different altogether from what he had thought it would be. . . . He scraped the earth off the top and began to loosen the earth around it. So intent was he on his task that he was unaware of Mr. Leicester's approach till he heard a shout and turned to see Mr. Leicester hanging over the barrier, his face crimson with rage, his eyes bulging. . . .

"Come back!" he shouted hoarsely. "Come *back*! You—you—you——" Words failed him. His mouth worked soundlessly in his purple face.

William straightened himself and looked from the bomb to Mr. Leicester . . . from Mr. Leicester to the bomb. . . .

"Come *back!*" said Mr. Leicester again. His voice was little more than a whisper, but it held even more fury than when it had been a shout.

William wiped his hands down his trousers.

"I'm all right," he said carelessly. "I'll fetch my tray thing if it starts explodin'. . . . But, I say, it's a

"COME BACK!" MR. LEICESTER SHOUTED HOARSELY.
"COME *BACK!* YOU—YOU—YOU——" WORDS
FAILED HIM.

jolly funny bomb. Come down an' have a look
at it."

Mr. Leicester's eyes, bulging and bloodshot with
emotion, went from William to the bomb . . . and
remained fixed on it. William had cleared all the earth
and debris away from it, and it lay there—large, round,
of a greyish hue. . . .

Suddenly William gave a shout.

"*Gosh!* I know what it is," he said.

In the same moment Mr. Leicester knew what it was, too.

It was the stone ball from the top of one of the brick piers that had formed the entrance gates of the Hall.

Pale now, but with his eyes still bulging, Mr. Leicester dived under the barrier and came down to join William in the crater. He stared at the bomb, stroked it, prodded it. . . . His face was a mask of incredulous horror.

"It *is*, isn't it?" said William.

Slowly Mr. Leicester turned to him. With an almost superhuman effort he had recovered something of his self-possession, something even of his normal manner. He looked shaken but master of himself.

"No need to—er—go about talking of this, my boy," he said. "No need to mention it at all. It would, in fact, be very wrong to—go about upsetting people's morale by—er—spreading rumours. There are very severe penalties for spreading rumours. I hope that you will remember that."

William looked at him in silence for a few moments. He was an intelligent boy and knew all about the process of face-saving. He was quite willing to help Mr. Leicester save his face, but he didn't see why he should do it for nothing.

"Then Joan an' her mother can go home to-morrow?" he said.

"Certainly," said Mr. Leicester graciously.

His eyes kept returning, as if drawn against his will, to the round smooth object at his feet.

"An' you'll come an' give your cinema show at her party, won't you?" said William with elaborate carelessness.

Mr. Leicester fixed a stern eye on him.

"You know quite well that I am not giving any such entertainments during the war," he said.

William gazed dreamily into the distance.

"I thought that if we had the cinema at the party," he said dreamily, "it'd be easier for me not to spread rumours."

Mr. Leicester gulped and swallowed. He looked long and hard at William. William continued to gaze dreamily into the distance. There was a silence . . . then Mr. Leicester yielded to the inevitable.

"Well, well, my boy," he said with a fairly good imitation of his pre-war geniality. "I—er—like to see young people enjoying themselves. If my duties permit, I will make an exception to my rule for this one occasion."

"An' if they don't," said William suavely, "we'll come an' fetch it, shall we? Joan's mother can manage it all right."

Again Mr. Leicester gulped and swallowed. Again he yielded to the inevitable.

"Just this once, then, my boy," he said graciously. "Just this once. It must never happen again, of course. And I will take for granted that you will not —er—spread rumours."

"No," promised William. "I won't spread rumours."

William had barely reached Miss Milton's house next morning when Mr. Leicester appeared, complete with all his District Warden's regalia. He looked stern and grim and aloof, as befitted one who has an important part to play in his country's destiny.

"I HAVE COME TO INFORM YOU, MRS. PARFITT," HE SAID
PORTENTOUSLY, "THAT THE UNEXPLODED BOMB HAS
BEEN—ER—DISPOSED OF."

"I have come to inform you, Mrs. Parfitt," he said
portentously, "that the unexploded bomb has been—
er—disposed of, and that you are at liberty to return
to your home at your convenience."

He avoided William's eye as he spoke.

"Oh how lovely!" said Joan. "Just in time for the
party! It *is* in time for the party, isn't it, Mummy?"

"Yes, dear," said Mrs. Parfitt joyfully. "It only gives us a day, but we can manage a grand party in a day."

Mrs. Parfitt would have liked to give a dozen parties to celebrate her release from Miss Milton. Only that morning Miss Milton had reproved her for drawing her bedroom curtains an inch further back on one side than on the other and had asked her to see that Joan did not put her hand on the baluster rail going up and down stairs, as she had found several finger marks on it.

"Ah, yes, the party," said Mr. Leicester with an expansive but somewhat mirthless smile. "This young man said that you wanted me to bring my kinematograph to it."

"Oh *please*, Mr. Leicester!" said Joan, clasping her hands and looking up at him beseechingly. "Oh *please*!"

Mr. Leicester gave a good imitation of a strong man melted by a child's pleading.

"Well, well," he said at last. "Well, well, well . . . I don't know. . . ."

"Oh, *please*!" said Joan again.

"Well," said Mr. Leicester. "Perhaps . . . just this once. . . . Mind, I'll never do it for you again and I'll never do it for anyone else at all—till after the war."

"That *is* kind of you, Mr. Leicester," said Mrs. Parfitt.

Joan was dancing about with joy.

"Oh, won't it be lovely!" she said. "Oh, *thank* you, Mr. Leicester."

"Isn't it kind of him, William?" said Mrs. Parfitt.

"Yes," agreed William. "Jolly kind."

"Er—not at all," murmured Mr. Leicester, fixing his eyes on the air just above William's head. "Not at all. Don't mention it. An exception, of course. . . . Not to be repeated."

"The bomb didn't explode, then?" said Mrs. Parfitt. "I suppose we'd have heard it here if it had done."

"Oh no," said Mr. Leicester, repeating the mirthless smile. "It didn't explode. It was—er—disposed of. The process," he went on hastily, "needs specialised knowledge, and the details, I am afraid, are too technical for you to understand."

Mrs. Parfitt looked at him, deeply impressed.

"How fortunate we are to have you for our warden!" she said.

* * * * *

Joan and William walked jauntily down the road, past the Lanes' house. At once Hubert Lane and a few friends, who were in the garden with him, popped their heads over the hedge.

"*Yah!*" they jeered. "Who's not havin' a party?"

"Well, who isn't?" said William innocently. "Joan is, an' we're all goin' to it an' we're goin' to have a jolly good time."

Hubert's mouth dropped open.

"*What!*" he said. "B-b-b-but what about the bomb?"

"Oh, that!" said William airily. "Goodness! Fancy you not havin' heard about that! It's been— disposed of. There isn't a bomb there any longer. Joan an' her mother's goin' back home at once."

Hubert's mouth remained open while he slowly digested this news.

"Well, anyway," he said, making a not very successful effort to recover himself. "Anyway, I bet yours won't be such a nice party as ours. I jolly well *bet* it won't."

"Don't you think so?" said William. He stopped to savour his piece of news before he brought it out. "Mr. Leicester's comin' to ours an' bringin' his cinema thing an' his films."

Hubert's eyes goggled. His face paled.

"N-n-n-not Mr. Leicester?" he said, as if pleading for mercy. "N-n-n-not his Mickey Mouse films?"

"'Course," said William cheerfully. "But he's not goin' to do it for anyone else. Only for Joan. . . . Come on, Joan."

They walked on, leaving a crestfallen silence behind them. Even the Hubert Laneites, pastmasters in the art of jeering, could think of no answering taunt.

As Joan and William walked on down the road, Joan looked suddenly at her companion. He was smiling to himself as at some private joke.

"William," she said, "you had *something* to do with it, hadn't you?"

"With what?" said William innocently.

"The bomb and the Mickey Mouse films and— everything."

"Well, just a bit," he admitted.

"Oh, William, do tell me."

He turned to her with a wink.

"I'll tell you after the war," he promised.

CHAPTER III

WILLIAM'S MIDSUMMER EVE

THE collection of "war souvenirs" had, of course, long been the chief interest of the younger inhabitants of the village. And here, as in many other fields, the rivalry between Hubert Lane and his followers, and William and his followers, showed itself.

Hubert was not particularly interested in his collection as a collector, but he was determined that it should outshine William's. And to Mrs. Lane, as usual, her darling's will was law. . . . Hubert wanted to have a better collection than those horrid Outlaws so he must have it. . . . And she didn't want her pet to tire himself out traipsing over the countryside for dirty bits of shrapnel, so she set to work to get them for him herself. She wrote to all her friends and relations in bombed areas who had children, offering large sums for collections of shrapnel and souvenirs, and paying postage in addition. By this means she soon got together the largest collection of shrapnel, copper driving-bands, pieces of incendiary bombs, bits of shell casing, nose-caps, time-fuses, and strips of land-mine parachute, for miles around. She labelled and polished and arranged them, and showed them off proudly to her friends as "Hubert's collection," while Hubert smiled his smug smile in the background. . . .

Different, indeed, was the lot of the Outlaws, who had to hunt the countryside for any small trophies they could find, whose mothers showed scant sympathy with their hobby, refusing it house room with a callous: "I won't have those nasty rusty things in the house, so take them out this minute."

In vain did they boast to Hubert: "We've got twenty pieces of shrapnel."

"Good Lord!" Hubert would counter scornfully. "We've got over two hundred."

Or: "I say, Hubert! Guess what we got this morning! Part of a nose-cap."

"Fancy that!" Hubert would sneer. "We've got six whole nose-caps."

What made things specially difficult for the Outlaws was that Farmer Jenks, on whose land they were in the habit of trespassing in their hunts for souvenirs, was these days in a particularly difficult humour. His only capable labourer had been "called up" and he was forced to employ a land girl. He hated girls—land or otherwise—so he took it out of everyone around him, particularly the land girl. She was a small slight girl called Katie, with red-gold curls and a friendly smile. The Outlaws liked her and, on the rare occasions when they had any sweets, generally called at the farm yard to offer her one. She was interested in the Outlaws' "collection" and would keep for them any pieces of shrapnel she found about the farm. She disliked Hubert Lane and his friends and refused to give them any. The result was that the Hubert Laneites classed her with the Outlaw gang and subjected her to the pleasant little attentions they reserved for their enemies, hiding behind the hedge to "catcall" at her and, in their more exuberant moments, throwing handfuls of mud at her as she went home in the evening to the cottage where she lodged. Katie was, however, of an optimistic and resilient nature and this did not worry her. Indeed, she occasionally amused herself by sallying forth from the farm and chasing the Hubert Laneites down the road with a pitchfork. . . . And she continued to give all aid she could to the Outlaws' "collection."

It was not, however, till she had been home for the week-end that she brought them a really sensational exhibit.

"I don't know whether it's any use to you," she said casually, "but an uncle of mine had it and he didn't want it, so I brought it along."

They stared incredulous, amazed, paralysed with delight, at a German bomb stick.

"Gosh!" gasped William. "Is it *really* for us?"

"'Course it is," said Katie, "if you want it, that is. I don't think worm Hubert's got one."

"Worm Hubert," as Katie called him, certainly hadn't got one. And "worm Hubert's" face, when he saw it, was a ludicrous mask of dismay.

"W-w-what's that?" he asked, peering over his garden hedge into the road, where the Outlaws passed in triumph, bearing aloft their trophy.

"Oh, it's jus' an' ordinary German bomb stick," said William carelessly.

"W-w-where d'you get it?" said Hubert.

"Katie gave it us."

"Has she got any more?"

"Oh no," said William. "They're very rare, but you can have a look at it."

Hubert had a look at it, examined it closely, jealously. . . .

"Bet I soon get one," he said. "Bet I get one by to-morrow."

But he didn't get one, despite the efforts of the entire Lane household. Mr. Lane asked all his business friends for one, Mrs. Lane wrote frantically to everyone she knew, offering large sums of money in exchange for one . . . but no German bomb stick arrived. The Hubert Lane collection, magnificent in every other way, rich in nose-caps and time-fuses and casings and copper driving-bands, remained without a German bomb stick. And the Outlaws made full use of their advantage.

"Got three more copper driving-bands," Hubert would shout triumphantly, and the Outlaws would retort:

"You've not got a German bomb stick."

"Got another nose-cap."

"You've not got a German bomb stick."

They took it about with them on their rambles through the woods and fields and on their trespassing expeditions. It was on one of these last that the tragedy happened. For Farmer Jenks met them coming out of the woods, knocked their heads together and—confiscated their bomb stick. He walked off with it, chuckling to himself (for he got a certain satisfaction out of his feud with the Outlaws), leaving them rubbing their heads and gazing after him in consternation. Their German bomb stick, the flower of their collection, their one defence against the jeers and taunts of their enemies! And the Hubert Laneites were not slow to realise the situation. They saw the

E

EXHILARATED BY THE DOWNFALL OF THEIR FOES, THE
HUBERT LANEITES GREW STILL MORE DARING.

Outlaws set off jauntily for their morning's activities
with their bomb stick, and saw them return crestfallen
without it.   They even had the good fortune to come

THEY APPROACHED KATIE AS SHE WAS DIGGING IN THE
POTATO FIELD.

upon a small boy who had seen the whole thing and
who reported it faithfully.

"Boxed their ears, 'e did, an' took that there stick
thing off of 'em."

The Hubert Laneites lost no time in profiting by
this turn of fortune's wheel.

"Yah! Who's not got a German bomb stick!
Yah! who had their German bomb stick took off 'em!"

They now enumerated their own collection with
restored and unbearable triumph. "We've got over

three hundred pieces of shrapnel an' seven nose-caps, lots more parachute cord an' eight driving-bands, and what've *you* got? *Yah!*"

Katie was as much distressed as the Outlaws by the tragedy.

"I'll have a good look for it," she said. "It ought to be somewhere about. If it is I'll get it back for you."

An exhaustive search of the farm buildings, however, revealed no German bomb stick.

"I'll have a look in the house if I get a chance," said Katie.

She got a chance and looked all over the house, still without result. She even, greatly daring, when Mrs. Jenks was shopping in Hadley and Farmer Jenks was safely in Six Acre Meadow, ran upstairs to search in the big front bedroom, with its mahogany furniture, enlarged photographs, crochet mats and the group of moth-eaten stuffed birds under a glass case, but without result.

"It just doesn't seem to be *anywhere*," she reported despairingly to the Outlaws.

And that wasn't the end. The second tragedy happened the next day. Exhilarated by the downfall of their foes, the Hubert Laneites grew still more daring. They approached Katie as she was digging in the potato field, and, smiling smugly, told her that Farmer Jenks wanted her in the big barn. Katie fell into the trap. She thrust her fork into the ground and went off to the big barn. Farmer Jenks was not there and Katie returned to find both the Hubert Laneites and her fork gone.

"The old horror's not found out about it yet," she told the Outlaws mournfully. "He checks up the tools on Saturday.   He'll be livid when he does.   He'll stop it out of my wages—and I shan't be able to go home for the week-end.   It's sickening, because I'd made a very special date."

"Don't you worry," said William grimly.   "We'll get it back for you.   We won't do anythin' else till we've *got* it back for you.   *An'* we'll get it back by Sat'day."

The Outlaws assembled in the old barn and took a solemn oath to that effect.   "We won't do anythin' else till we've got 'em both back an' we'll get 'em back by Sat'day," asseverated William, and the other three agreed.

The double task was, however, easier to undertake than to carry out.   Daring raids upon the farm and its outbuildings merely confirmed what Katie had already told them.   The bomb stick had apparently vanished into air.

"I bet he's buried it somewhere," said William.   "I *bet* he has."

"No, he wouldn't ,"said Ginger.   "He wouldn't do that.   He's planted every *inch* of ground with onions an' things same as the gov'nment told him to."

"I bet he's sold it."

"I bet he's not.   He doesn't know the sort of people what want things like that.   He only knows the sort of people what want pigs an' corn an' stuff."

"I bet he's taken it to someone else's house to hide."

"No, he hasn't.   People would've seen him takin' it.   We'd've known. . . ."

"Well, then, it must be here somewhere," said Ginger.   "It jus' must."

"An' that ole scarecrow seems to be laughin' at us all the time," grumbled William, looking at the scarecrow

that had stood in the middle of the field next the
farm for as long as the Outlaws could remember. It
wore a battered old slouch hat and a cape-like ulster
that had, many years ago, adorned Farmer Jenks'
person. Certainly it seemed to flap its arms derisively
in the breeze as it watched the Outlaws' futile attempts
to find their missing treasure.

The hunt for the fork was no more satisfactory.
Raids into the Lanes' greenhouse, toolshed and con-
servatory met with no other result than a painful
encounter with the Lanes' gardener (a misanthropic
embittered man, who looked on all boys as so many
Huberts and hated them accordingly), and a narrow
shave when Mr. Lane appeared suddenly at the gate
by which they were making their escape and only
missed them because he tried to catch them all at
once.

The search, however, had convinced them that the
missing fork was nowhere in the Lanes' outbuildings.
The Outlaws would have abandoned the search as
hopeless if it had not been for William. William was
definitely of the bulldog type. Having once taken
hold, he didn't let go. . . .

"No," he said firmly, "we're goin' to do it. We
said we'd do it an' we're *goin'* it do it. An' we're goin'
to do it by Sat'day."

"Well, we've tried," protested Ginger. "We've
looked everywhere an' they aren't anywhere."

"Well, then, we'll start all over again," said William.

"How? We'll jus' look again an' they still won't
be there."

"We've gotter start a different way."

"What diff'rent way?"

"Well—we won't try 'em both at once. We'll fix which we'll find first an' we'll—well, we'll jus' *find* it."

"Well, then, which?"

"Well—the fork. I bet we oughter start findin' Katie's fork before we start findin' our own bomb stick."

"Don't see how we're goin' to find either of 'em," said Ginger morosely. "We've tried hard enough."

"I tell you we've gotter start lookin' a diff'rent *way*," said William impatiently.

"What way?"

"Oh, be quiet for a bit," said William. "I'm tryin' to *think*."

"We've looked everywhere an' it's not there. It's no use startin' lookin' everywhere again. It still won't be there."

"No," said William slowly, "we've gotter make Hubert give it us back."

"But he won't," objected Douglas. "We've asked him an' he jus' pretends he doesn't know what we're talkin' about. No one *saw* 'em take it, you know. An' it's no good tryin' to *make* him give it us back. If we *touch* him he gets his father to write to our fathers, an' we get into a row."

"No," said William, "we won't do it that way. We'll make it so's Hubert *wants* to give it us back."

"Dunno how you'll do that," grumbled Henry.

"Nor do I jus' now," admitted William, "but I bet I'll think of a way."

As he passed the cornfield next to Farmer Jenks' farm on his way home, the scarecrow again seemed to flap his arms at him in mockery.

"Oh, shut up," muttered William impatiently, for

he hadn't yet thought of a way and was beginning to feel somewhat less optimistic about his ability to do so. "Shut up flappin' about an' makin' fun of people! Well, I bet *you* couldn't think of a way. I jolly well *bet* you couldn't."

The scarecrow seemed to wave its arms still more derisively. The exasperated William took up a stone from the road and hurled it at the mocking figure. He missed it by several feet and walked on in disgust.

"SHUT UP, FLAPPIN' ABOUT AN' MAKIN' FUN OF PEOPLE!" MUTTERED WILLIAM IMPATIENTLY.

"Can't even hit an ole scarecrow!" he muttered in angry self-abasement. "Can't even do *that*."

But it was the scarecrow that gave him his first idea. It didn't come to him at once. It didn't come to him, in fact, till he was going to bed. . . . He happened to glance at the calendar on his mother's writing table after supper and noticed without much interest the words "Longest Day" against next Saturday.

"Longest day?" he said.

"Yes, dear," said Mrs. Brown. "They call it Midsummer Day, and the day before it is called Midsummer Eve. There are all sorts of superstitions connected with it."

"What sorts?" said William, more from an ineradicable propensity for asking questions than because he really wanted to know.

"I'm a little vague about it, dear, but I think that fairies are supposed to have special powers and that sort of thing."

"Why?" said William.

"Oh really, William, I don't know. Do stop asking questions. I'm busy."

William went out into the garden. He was looking very thoughtful. The word "fairies" had struck a chord in his mind.

Fairies. . . . Hubert Lane believed in fairies. More than once in the past William had played on that particular weakness. Could he play on it again?

He was so quiet that evening that his mother looked at him anxiously.

"Are you feeling ill, dear?" she asked.

William abandoned his expression of deep thoughtfulness, which, to do Mrs. Brown justice, always suggested acute nausea.

"Ill? Me?" he asked. "Gosh! I don't get enough to eat to feel ill on these days."

Perhaps it was a guilty conscience, thought Mrs. Brown.

"William, have you been at the store cupboard again?"

Injured innocence radiated from William's freckled countenance.

"Me?" he said. "Been at the store cupboard? Gosh!" bitterly. "You don't give me a chance these days. It's always locked."

"What are you thinking of, then?" asked Mrs. Brown.

William assumed an expression of imbecile sweetness.

"Fairies," he said.

"Don't be silly, dear," said Mrs. Brown.

But William *was* thinking about fairies, and he continued to think about them all that evening. . . . By the time he went to sleep his plans were fully laid.

He happened to run into Hubert Lane as Hubert was coming out of the sweet shop in the village early on Friday. Hubert visited the sweet shop every morning in order to buy what small allowance of sweets the shop-keeper had at his disposal. Mrs. Lane provided her son with large sums of money for the purpose and told the shopman to keep any sweets he got for Hubert because he was used to eating as many as he wanted and it would be a shock to his system if he had to stop. The shopkeeper said nothing, but it was noticed that often, when he had told Hubert there were no sweets available, he would produce them for the Outlaws.

On seeing William, Hubert hastily slipped a bag of humbugs into his pocket and transferred a large bulge from one side of his mouth to the middle. Even in the days of peace and plenty Hubert had never been known to "hand round" his sweets.

"Hello, Hubert," said William in a voice that was obviously friendly—even conciliatory.

The look of apprehension left Hubert's face, and he abandoned his half-formed project of dodging back into the shop for safety. The Outlaws evidently knew when they were beaten, he thought with an inward chuckle. Or else they had forgotten the whole affair. . . . The short memory of the Outlaws for insults and injuries was always surprising Hubert. He himself never forgot one till he had avenged it to his satisfaction.

"Hello," he muttered guardedly.

"You goin' home?" said William. "I'm goin' along your way. . . ."

The two boys set off down the road.

"You're not worryin' any more about that ole fork?" Hubert couldn't help saying through his humbug.

"What fork?" said William blankly. Then, as if with difficulty remembering something in the remote past, "Oh, that. . . . Gosh no! 'S'no good worryin' over that."

"Well, it hadn't anythin' to do with us," said Hubert. "She jus' lost it, I s'pose."

He accompanied the words with a malicious little grin, but William did not seem to notice it.

"'Course," he agreed. Then, conversationally: "Midsummer Eve's to-day, isn't it?"

"I know," agreed Hubert, lulled into a sense of false security and sucking his humbug openly. There was a triumphant swagger in his walk. He had, he considered, scored off the Outlaws at last. The fork was safely hidden in the box-room at home behind a pile of trunks, and the Outlaws had in any case no proof that it was he who had taken it. And Farmer Jenks wasn't likely to give them the German bomb stick back. Better rub it in a bit more. . . .

"Pity havin' that bomb stick of yours took off you," he said.

"Yes, wasn't it?" agreed William.

"Don't suppose you'll ever see it again."

"'Fraid not," said William.

"Doesn't leave you much of a collection, does it?"

"No," said William.

"I got another nose-cap this mornin'. I've got ten now. You've only got one, haven't you, an' that's all bashed up?"

"Yes," agreed William.

A discerning boy would have been put on his guard by the unusual humility of William's manner, but Hubert was not a discerning boy. He continued to gloat and throw his weight about for about five more minutes, uttering insults, and taunts that normally William would not have endured. But William endured them, though once or twice it might have been noticed that he clenched his teeth and fists. When Hubert paused for breath, he introduced the subject of Midsummer Eve again.

"All sorts of funny tales about it," he said. "Animals talkin' an' people gettin' their wishes an' such like."

"I know," said Hubert earnestly. "They're true, too, but they don't happen till midnight an' we're in bed by then, so we can't see it."

"That one about scarecrows is s'posed to happen earlier, you know," said William.

"Scarecrows?" said Hubert with interest. "I never heard one about scarecrows."

"Oh, there's nothin' in those ole tales," said William contemptuously. "I don't believe any of 'em."

"No, but what's the one about scarecrows?" demanded Hubert, taking another humbug out of his pocket and slipping it into his mouth. "I never heard one about scarecrows."

"Well, you bet there's nothin' in it."

"No, but what is it?" demanded Hubert, his curiosity whetted beyond endurance. "What *is* it?"

"Dunno if I remember it right," said William, "but they're s'posed to come alive jus' after dark an' come to anyone what's stole anythin' out of their fields durin' the year an' get it back off them."

Hubert paled.

"G-g-get it back off them?" he stammered.

"Yes," said William carelessly. "They leave the person what stole it in a jolly nasty mess, too. They've got the strength of ten men when they come alive, scarecrows have. Well, I know I wouldn't like to be knocked about by a scarecrow come alive with the strength of ten men."

"The s-s-s-s-strength of ten men?"

"Yes, or it might've been twenty."

"I don't believe it," said Hubert, but looking like a boy in the grip of a nightmare.

"I don't either," agreed William. "I don't believe a word of any of those soppy ole fairy tales. It wouldn't come to me, anyway, 'cause I've not stolen anything off a field. An' you haven't either, have you?"

"N-n-no," said Hubert hastily. "No, 'course I've not. *'Course* I've not."

"I think those ole tales are all silly," said William scornfully. "People must've been bats to believe in 'em. We've got a bit more sense now. 'Bout half-past ten the scarecrows are s'posed to come alive. Never heard anything so cracked, did you? Well, here's your house, Hubert. . . . Nearly tea time, isn't it? I'll be gettin' on home."

Hubert walked slowly up his garden path. His face was pale and thoughtful. Having reached the front door and realising that he was safe from reprisal, he recovered himself sufficiently to bawl: "Yah! who got their bomb stick took off 'em? What happened to Katie's fork? *Yah!*" after William's retreating figure. But the last question evidently roused an unpleasant memory, and he went into the house looking so pallid and troubled that his mother rang up the chemist for a tonic. . . .

Hubert lay in bed, gazing at the clock on his mantelpiece. It seemed to have an irresistible fascination for him. He tried to close his eyes and go to sleep but he couldn't. He kept opening them to look at the clock. Ten o'clock . . . five past ten . . . ten past ten . . . quarter past ten . . . twenty past ten . . . twenty-five past ten . . . half past ten. . . . He had to do it. He simply couldn't help himself. He slipped out of bed,

opened the window curtains and peeped out. . . . And
then—his blood froze, his eyes dilated with horror and
his plump pale face turned a delicate green. For,
coming in at the gate, was the scarecrow from Farmer
Jenks' field. The broad-brimmed hat met the collar
of the large ulster, as it had always done. The arms
were stiffly out-stretched, the cape-like sleeves flapped,
it walked with a rigid, unnatural gait. Beyond all
possible doubt it was Farmer Jenks' scarecrow, and it
was coming to the house for the fork that Hubert had
taken from the field. . . . He remembered what

COMING IN AT THE GATE WAS THE SCARECROW FROM
FARMER JENKS' FIELD.

William had said: "They leave the person what stole it in a jolly nasty mess. . . . They've got the strength of ten men . . . it may be twenty men. . . ."

Bleating with terror, Hubert darted out of his bedroom and into the box-room next door. Frantically and still bleating, he burrowed behind the pile of trunks and brought out the fork. Fortunately for William, it happened that an eminent politician with a particularly resonant voice was speaking on the wireless that evening, and hid their son's bleatings and burrowings from parental ears downstairs. In a few seconds Hubert had returned to his bedroom and pulled back the curtain. The scarecrow had advanced almost to the front door. Glancing up from beneath the shadow of the hat, William saw Hubert's face like the face of a panic-stricken sheep at the window. Then the window was flung up and the fork came out, missing William's head by a fraction of an inch.

Stooping stiffly, mechanically, as he imagined a scarecrow would stoop, he picked it up and set off with his jerky unnatural gait back towards the road. Hubert tumbled into bed and drew the clothes high over his head, still bleating. . . .

Actually William was hardly less scared than Hubert himself. He had not realised till he came to carry out his plan how beset with perils it was. First there was getting up after he had officially gone to bed, dressing and escaping from the house, then there was going to the field where the scarecrow was, and donning its garments when at any moment Farmer Jenks might have appeared, then there was that hazardous approach to the Lanes' house, when at any moment Mr. and Mrs. Lane might have looked out of the window or sallied

forth from the door. . . . Then, having secured the
fork, there was the still more hazardous return. . . .
But Fate was kind to William, and all the people
who might have confronted him on his adventurous career were sitting by their wireless fervently
drinking in the words of the eminent politician. . . .
Fate was indeed more than kind. It seemed as if it
were anxious to make up to him for its late neglect.
For, as he was replacing the upright on which the
scarecrow's clothes were draped, William suddenly
stopped and looked at it intently. It was strangely
familiar. It was, in fact, nothing else than the German
bomb stick. . . . Farmer Jenks had had a brain wave.
He had put it, he thought, where the Outlaws would
never find it, however hard they searched. . . . Lying
near was the brown handle that had originally formed
the upright. William set it up, fixed the cross stick
upon it, replaced hat and ulster, then, carrying fork in
one hand, bomb stick in the other, started off homeward.

As he crept across the hall and up the stairs, the
voice of the eminent politician was upraised sten-
toriously in his peroration, drowning even the creaking
of the middle stair and William's sudden stumble on
reaching the landing. . . .

Next morning the Outlaws, headed by William,
marched past Hubert Lane's house in a procession of
triumph. William carried the bomb stick and Ginger
the fork. Hubert's face popped up suddenly over the
hedge. It was a little paler than usual, for he had had
a broken night, disturbed by strange dreams.

He stared at the triumphal procession in amazement.
His eyes goggled, his mouth fell open.

F

"We've found our bomb stick, you see, Hubert," said William pleasantly.

"W-w-w-where?" gasped Hubert.

"Oh, we jus' found it," said William airily. "We thought we'd have a look for it, so we did an' found it."

"I'll give you all my nose-caps for it," said Hubert in almost tearful pleading.

"No you won't, 'cause we don't want 'em," said William. "And we found that fork Katie lost, too," he went on.

Hubert's gaze goggled at the fork and for some moments the power of speech deserted him.

"W-w-w-where?" he managed to bring out at last.

"Funny thing!" said William ruminatively. "We found it by that ole scarecrow in Farmer Jenks' field. Can't think how it got there."

Hubert's teeth chattered. His hair seemed to rise up on his head.

"G-g-g-golly!" he stuttered. "F-f-f-fancy that!"

"Like to have a look at it?" said Ginger, making as if to hand it over the hedge.

Hubert gave a squeal of terror.

"No, no. Take it away," he said. "Take it away."

"A' right," said Ginger. "Come on, William. Let's get on."

Waving fork and bomb stick in the air, its voices raised in unmelodious shouts of triumph, the procession passed on its way. . . .

CHAPTER IV

JOAN TO THE RESCUE

THE Outlaws first saw Madame Montpelimar at
the Bring and Buy Sale organised by Mrs. Bott
in aid of the Red Cross. They had heard of her before,
of course. She had come to the village about a week
ago as the chief attraction of an American Tea
given by Mrs. Flowerdew in aid of her War Comforts
Fund. Madame Montpelimar was a fortune-teller.
She told fortunes by crystal, cards, palms, stars—but
principally by sheer bluff. And she got away with it.
A few discreet questions at a few of the local shops on
the way from the station to the scene of her labours
generally gave her some leading ideas on the various
inhabitants, and she made the most of them.

She was an expert, too, at drawing pieces of information from her clients about themselves and serving
them up a few minutes later, so spiced and garnished
that the client was amazed by her powers. "She's
simply wonderful . . ." they said when they had paid
their two and six and emerged from her little tent. "She
told me all about my operation and my husband's work."

Some, of course, were less impressed than others.
Mrs. Flowerdew, who had engaged her on impulse from
an advertisement for her American Tea and regretted it
as soon as she saw her, openly said that she was a

fraud. Mrs. Bott, on the other hand, said that she was "so physic (by which that lady meant psychic) she could see right into the middle of next week." For Madame Montpelimar had learnt all that it was necessary to learn about the lady of the Hall on her way from the station, and she took a good deal of trouble over her "fortune." Mrs. Bott was a short-tempered, overbearing, kind-hearted, pig-headed woman, shrewd enough in practical matters but extremely credulous in the realms of the occult—or the "physic" as she called it. She believed that she herself possessed "physic" powers above the average, and was always a ready victim to anyone who cared to play on this weakness.

She came out of Madame Montpelimar's curtained recess looking pale and shaken.

"She told me things I 'ardly knew myself," she said in an awestruck voice.

Madame Montpelimar, besides telling Mrs. Bott various authentic details of her past history that she had gleaned at the post office and from other clients, had told her that she was an "old soul" (which had slightly affronted that lady till she discovered the meaning of the expression), gifted with striking psychic powers that only needed development.

"You ought to have them developed," Madame Montpelimar had said earnestly. "You could easily acquire the power of clairvoyance and clairaudience with only a little training. But, of course, you need careful training. You should have an expert with you all the time at first. Someone who has the Power and whom you can trust."

And so for the next few weeks Madame Montpelimar

was comfortably installed at the Hall in the capacity of psychic teacher to its mistress. She drove with Mrs. Bott through the village in the Rolls Royce, she shared with Mrs. Bott the far from meagre meals that even in war time Mrs. Bott managed to procure. She wore the satisfied smile of one who has been on her beam ends and has found a mug in the nick of time. . . .

In appearance she was small and stout and dark and frowzy. She had a sallow wrinkled gipsy-looking skin, she wore dingy and ancient garments that seemed to float about her like cobwebs, and she had a wealth of dull brown hair elaborately frizzed in front and done in a large "bun" of greasy-looking coils behind.

"She looks just like a witch," said Mrs. Flowerdew, "and a witch who needs a good wash at that."

"Of course, she's an adventuress," said everyone.

"Pity Mr. Bott's away," they added.

Mr. Bott gave in to most of his wife's caprices, but even he, they felt, would have drawn the line at Madame Montpelimar.

Madame Montpelimar found the task of training her pupil comparatively easy. Mrs. Bott was given to dreams of a particularly illogical and senseless description, generally inspired by the events of the previous day, and Madame Montpelimar interpreted them as miracles of "clairvoyance" such as only an "old soul" could have attained. She encouraged Mrs. Bott's "intuitions" too and, there again, generally managed to interpret them to that lady's complete satisfaction. Her own reputation she sustained with ease, for Mrs. Bott seemed quite satisfied with such vague messages from the spirit world as: "Hope ever," "You are one of us," "Do not be discouraged. We are all helping

you," and others of the same sort. She even
swallowed: "We are all amazed at the progress you
are making," from a defunct Eastern seer who,
according to Madame Montpelimar, only sent messages
on very important occasions.

The financial side of the question, however, was less
satisfactory. Beneath Mrs. Bott's foolishness and
credulity there was a hard if deeply hidden vein of
common sense, left over from the days before she had
nothing to do but spend her husband's money, and
this hard vein of common sense suggested that Madame
Montpelimar was amply repaid by her board and
lodging for the hours of work she was actually putting
in. Madame Montpelimar produced dreams, visions,
spirit messages in abundance to the effect that Mrs.
Bott should hand over large sums of money to her
instructress in return for the wonderful "training" she
was receiving, and indeed for the benefit of humanity
in general, but at that point Mrs. Bott always became
evasive.

"I'll 'ave to leave that till Botty comes 'ome," she
would say, and Madame Montpelimar, in view of her
oft-expressed indifference to material things, had no
choice but to acquiesce. At first the luxury in which
she now lived seemed, indeed, sufficient repayment for
her trouble, but gradually she began to grow restive.
She couldn't stay here indefinitely (in fact, without
much exercise of clairvoyance she foresaw that her
visit would terminate abruptly with the return of Mr.
Bott), and if she hadn't made any more out of it than
a few meals and rides in a car she was, she told herself,
a bigger fool than she'd thought. She stopped giving
Mrs. Bott spirit messages demanding money (one could

overdo that sort of thing, as she'd learnt by experience) and began instead to watch her opportunity. She prided herself on being a woman who never let an opportunity slip.

And then came Mrs. Bott's Bring and Buy Sale in aid of the Red Cross. Madame Montpelimar was ensconced in her comfortable little alcove, with the crystal ball as the main attraction, behind a large placard: Know Your Future. The Famous Clair- voyante, Madame Montpelimar. Two and six each; but only a sprinkling of people—mostly strangers to the district—visited her. The others crowded round the loaded stalls, bringing and buying with unabating zeal, but Madame Montpelimar's alcove remained unpatronised.

"Aren't you going to have your fortune told by Madame Montpelimar, Mrs. Flowerdew?" said Mrs. Bott agressively.

"No, thank you, Mrs. Bott," said Mrs. Flowerdew, "I don't think she's very good, and in any case I'm not interested in that sort of thing."

The truth was gradually borne in upon Mrs. Bott that her protégée was being ostracised. This was, she considered, an insult not only to her protégée but to her own psychic powers.

Mrs. Bott was not a woman to suffer an insult meekly. Her usually rubicund cheeks became brick red, her small eyes hard and bright. She stood in the middle of the room glaring round her, breathing noisily, looking for trouble. . . . And she found it.

It happened that Mrs. Brown had a bad cold and could not come to the Sale, so she had sent William in her place. He was to take her contribution (a tea cosy sent her by a cousin last Christmas) and in order to recompense him for performing this uncongenial task she had given him two and six to spend on himself.

"Of course, you may not find anything you like . . ." she had warned him.

"*May* not!" William echoed bitterly. "They'll be all rotten ole traycloths an' tea cosies an' babies' frocks. I know 'em."

"Never mind, dear," Mrs. Brown had consoled him. "If you can't find anything you want yourself, get something for me and I'll buy it from you."

But much to William's surprise he did find something he wanted. He found—lying carelessly between a pokerwork photograph frame and a hideous green vase, almost hidden by a baby's knitted jacket—the most magnificent penknife he had ever seen in his life. It had four blades, a corkscrew, a file, and a gadget for getting stones out of a horse's hoof. And it was marked two and six. William pounced upon it, his eyes shining with eagerness, and retired to a corner of the room to examine it. He opened the blades one by one. . . . He caressed them lovingly. The spike for getting stones out of a horse's hoof he was specially pleased with. He'd never had an opportunity to use one yet, but it might arise at any moment, and he was glad to think that he would be equal to it. He ran his finger tentatively along the blades. They seemed sharp, all right. The temptation to test his prize at once was irresistible. . . . He carried under his arm a stick that he had taken from the hedge on his way to the Sale for use as a walking stick. He stood—screened from onlookers, as he thought, in a corner of the room —and made a few tentative cuts at the end of his

stick with his knife. Yes, it was a jolly good penknife. . . . It was upon this sight that Mrs. Bott's
angry eye fell as it roved the room in search of trouble.
She bore down upon him like a warship in full steam.

"'Ow *dare* you go makin' that mess on my nice
clean floor, William Brown?" she stormed. "Give me
that there penknife this minute."

William looked down at the little heap of shavings
at his feet. Actually it did not seem such a heinous
crime. The carpet had been rolled up for the occasion,
and the bare floor was already littered with bits of paper
and string and various other flotsam and jetsam of the
Bring and Buy Sale, but Mrs. Bott wanted an outlet
for her anger and William provided one. She had even
begun to bear down on him before she realised what he
was doing. Whatever William Brown was doing anywhere was sure to be wrong. . . .

"Give me that there penknife this minute," she
repeated, "an' clear out of 'ere."

"But I've only just bought it an' I paid two and six
for it," objected William. "I'll clear the mess up.
There isn't much. I——"

Mrs. Bott snatched the penknife out of his hand,
turned her back on him and was already half way
across the room.

William stared after her, paralysed for a moment by
indignation.

"I say, you can't take my——" he began, then
realised that no one was listening to him. He pushed
his way through the crowd of bringers and buyers till
he reached Mrs. Bott.

"I say," he said sternly, "I paid two and six for
that penknife an'——"

Mrs. Bott swung round on him. Her progress through the room had shown her Madame Montpelimar sitting alone in her curtained alcove, boycotted by bringers and buyers alike. She had even caught sight of Mrs. Monks and Mrs. Flowerdew obviously discussing the lady with expressions of contemptuous amusement. She was in no mood, therefore, to listen to William's explanations and excuses.

"Di'n't you 'ear me tell you to get out of 'ere?" she stormed. "You get out of 'ere this minute or I'll——" A large upraised hand threatened a speedy descent upon his ear, and William, surrendering to superior forces, carried out a successful strategic retreat.

He walked home despondently. . . . The penknife, now that fate had so cruelly snatched it from him, seemed even more desirable than it had seemed in actual possession.

"Just a few bits of wood," he muttered indignantly, "'mong all that mess! As if it'd make any diff'rence! Why cun't she've took *their* things off them—their ole tea cosies an' such like? They'd made jus' as much mess as me. It's not *fair*. . . ."

His mother was, as he had foreseen, unsympathetic.

"Well, William, I'm sure it serves you right. No, I know I wasn't there, but I know what a nuisance you can make of yourself. I'm very glad that Mrs. Bott did take it away from you and I hope it will be a lesson to you."

But William's resentment waxed higher the more he thought over the incident. A few bits of wood on a floor that was all messed up, anyway!

His resentment became a determination to retrieve his property at all costs.

"A crim'nal, that's what she is," he muttered fiercely. "I wouldn't go to another ole Sale at her house—not even if"—he sought for the most unlikely contingency possible and added—"she wanted me to."

He turned his steps back to the Hall, entered the gates and made his way up towards the house in the shadow of the shubbery. The Bring and Buy Sale was evidently over now. The big drawing-room, where it had been held, was empty except for a few maids who were sweeping the floor in a half-hearted fashion. . . . William made his way round to the side, where Mrs. Bott's bedroom was. He could still see no signs of life. As a matter of fact, the servants were washing up the Bring and Buy tea things or clearing the big drawing-room; Mrs. Bott was resting in her "boodwor" upstairs (Mrs. Bott in her youth had read novels in which the heroines had boudoirs and the first thing she had done on occupying the Hall was to set aside a small room near her bedroom for that purpose); and Madame Montpelimar was resting in the small drawing-room downstairs, renewing her forces and drawing out a plan of campaign. The events of the afternoon had shown her that such small local influence as she had was on the wane. In any case she was fed up with Mrs. Bott and the Hall and the village and everything connected with them. She would have liked to have packed her things and gone then and there, but professional pride prevented her. She'd never been got the better of by a mug yet and she wasn't going to start now. She'd taken for granted that she would make enough out of Mrs. Bott to keep her in comfort for the rest of the year and all she'd got was her keep, a few drives in a car, and hours upon hours of boredom.

She wasn't going till she'd done a bit better than that. She'd tried dreams, visions, mystic voices, spirit visitants—but all in vain. . . . She was wondering what to try next when she saw, from the shadow of the curtain where she was sitting, a small boy cautiously approach the house and begin to climb up a drain pipe screened by a climbing rose-tree. She recognised the boy. It was the boy whose penknife Mrs. Bott had taken at the Sale. Obviously he was going to retrieve his penknife. For the temptation of Mrs. Bott's open bedroom window and the drain pipe so conveniently near it had proved too much for William. The wide open window showed that Mrs. Bott (whose dislike of fresh air was notorious) was not in the room, and the drain pipe seemed to call him urgently to reconnoitre. . . . There was just a chance that Mrs Bott might have put the penknife down in her bedroom in some accessible position. It was worth trying, anyway. . . . He didn't want tamely to go home without having even made an attempt to get his penknife back. . . .

The garden was empty. There seemed to be no one about anywhere. . . . He swarmed quickly up the pipe. . . . The bedroom was empty. He stepped over the sill, looked about him, then gave a gasp of relief and joy. Yes, there on the dressing-table, side by side with a large diamond brooch, was his penknife. . . . He darted across the room to it, slipped it into his pocket, and slid down the drain pipe again. . . .

Meantime, Madame Montpelimar had not been idle. She was a woman whose wits worked quickly in an emergency and she was well practised in emergencies. The boy had gone to Mrs. Bott's bedroom for his penknife, which Madame Montpelimar happened to know was on the dressing-table. Madame Montpelimar happened to know, too, that the diamond brooch was on the dressing-table. She had seen Mrs. Bott put both of them down when she came in from the Bring and Buy Sale. If she could get possession of the diamond brooch and manage to lay the blame of its disappearance on the boy, she'd feel that she could leave the place with her future secured for some considerable time and the satisfaction of having got her own back. She'd have paid Mrs. Bott out for the hours of boredom and for her deafness to all her requests for money. Mrs. Bott was very careless with her jewellery, and only the knowledge that she would inevitably fall under suspicion had prevented Madame Montpelimar from helping herself to some of it before now. . . . Her fingers, in fact, had fairly itched when she saw her hostess leave diamond brooches and pearl necklaces carelessly about in bedroom and "boodwor." But Madame Montpelimar and the police had met on more than one occasion previously, and she was reluctant to renew the acquaintance. This, however, was an opportunity not to be missed. And Madame Montpelimar did not miss it. . . . She laid her plan of campaign quickly.

She hastened out to the garden in the front of the house and called a gardener who was working at the back. . . . He was a young man and obeyed her summons fairly quickly. Madame Montpelimar, keeping the corner of her eye on Mrs. Bott's bedroom window, through which William had vanished, asked the gardener the name of a shrub in which she said she was interested. She asked about its habits, its culture,

"LOOK!" SHE SAID. "WHAT ON EARTH . . .? IT'S A *BOY*. CATCH HIM AND I'LL GO AND TELL MRS. BOTT."

the best time to plant it, how to prune it. . . . From the corner of her eye she saw William emerge from the window, but it wasn't till he had almost reached the ground that, with a sudden exclamation of surprise and horror, she called the gardener's attention to him.

"Look!" she said. "What on earth . . .? It's a *boy*. Catch him and I'll go and tell Mrs. Bott."

William, as she had meant him to, heard the sharp exclamation, leapt to the ground and set off through the bushes, pursued by the gardener. Madame Montpelimar waited to see that William was making good his escape before she ran into the house, up the stairs, and along the passage to Mrs. Bott's bedroom. Yes, there was the diamond brooch. . . . She slipped it into her pocket, then went quickly on to Mrs. Bott's "boodwor." In her eagerness to give the impression of having come straight from the garden she went indeed a little too quickly, slipping down the two steps that led into the "boodwor" and landing at the feet of the astonished Mrs. Bott.

Mrs. Bott sat up on her pink brocade sofa (all the heroines had pink brocade sofas in their "boodwors") and clutched her lace-trimmed negligée about her (the heroines all had lace-trimmed negligées, too).

"'Ere!" she said. "What's all this?"

"Never mind me," gasped Madame Montpelimar, surreptitiously making sure that the brooch was still in her pocket. "Go quickly. A boy's been into your bedroom. I was in the garden talking to the gardener when suddenly I saw him coming down the drain pipe from your bedroom. It was that boy you took the penknife from. I sent the gardener after him and I came upstairs as quickly as I could to tell you."

"That boy!" groaned Mrs. Bott, putting her plump little feet to the floor and slipping them into the shoes she had taken off a few minutes ago. "'E's in every bit of mischief there is in this 'ere village. In prison's where he ought to be an' the sooner 'e goes there the better. Where d'you say 'e'd been?"

"Your bedroom," said Madame Montpelimar, getting up from the floor and limping to a chair. "At least, I think he must have been there because he was coming down that drain pipe by the rose tree. It doesn't lead anywhere else. And your window was open. . . . Probably the gardener's caught him by now."

Mrs. Bott rose slowly to her feet.

"S'pose I'd better go an' see what mischief 'e's been up to. Layin' some booby trap, I'll be bound. Made me an apple pie bed, like as not. I wouldn't put it past him."

She hobbled from the room—to return a few minutes later, looking white and shaken.

"Would you believe it," she gasped, sinking down again upon the pink brocade sofa, "the little devil's gone an' stole me diamond brooch!"

"Oh, Mrs. Bott!" said Madame Montpelimar. "Never! I simply won't believe it."

"Then come and see with your own eyes," said Mrs. Bott. "Gone. Clean gone. That's what it is."

"But are you sure you left it there?" said Madame Montpelimar.

"'Course I am," said Mrs. Bott, "I put it down there along with the penknife. 'E's taken them both. I always said that boy was little more nor less than a criminal an' now I've proved it."

"It's probably dropped down behind the dressing-table," said Madame Montpelimar. "I can't believe that a child like that would steal a valuable piece of jewellery."

"You don't know 'im like what I do," said Mrs.

Bott darkly. "At the bottom of every piece of mischief in this village 'e's been ever since I can remember. I've always said 'e'd end up in jail."

Madame Montpelimar rose slowly to her feet and accompanied her hostess along the passage to her bedroom. She walked slowly and painfully. A horrible suspicion was forming itself in her mind that in that headlong entrance into the boudoir she had sprained her ankle. She had meant to make a quick get-away with the goods to-night. Get-aways were child's play to Madame Montpelimar. A vision of a friend in trouble or a spirit voice calling her to some urgent piece of psychic work on the other side of England, had often saved her in the nick of time. But a sprained ankle would complicate matters. . . .

"There!" said Mrs. Bott, pointing dramatically to the dressing-table. "There they were, the two of 'em. I put the penknife down there an' I took off me dress an' put me diamond brooch next the penknife. I'll take me dyin' oath to it. An' I slipped on me negligée an' told Marie to leave the brooch there as I'd want to wear it with me mauve chiffon for dinner."

Mrs. Bott's maid Marie, summoned, corroborated the story. She had helped Mrs. Bott take off her dress and put on her negligée, had seen Mrs. Bott into the boudoir, returned to tidy up the bedroom, and put out the mauve chiffon that was to adorn Mrs. Bott's ample person at dinner, and had departed, leaving penknife and diamond brooch, side by side, on the dressing-table. No one had entered the room since then—till Madame Montpelimar and the gardener had seen William Brown climbing furtively down the drain pipe from the open bedroom window.

G

At this point the panting gardener arrived. He hadn't been able to catch the boy but he'd recognised him. It was that there William Brown. . . .

Mrs. Bott pursed her small tight mouth till it almost vanished into her puffy cheeks.

"Well, 'e gives me that there brooch back or 'e goes to jail. I'll tell 'is father so this very evenin'."

Madame Montpelimar sank on to the bed, her face twisted into lines of pain.

"I—I think I've sprained my ankle," she moaned.

*   *   *   *   *

"But Mrs. Bott," protested Mrs. Brown aghast, "William couldn't *possibly* have stolen your diamond brooch."

"Well, 'e could an' 'e 'as done," snapped Mrs. Bott. "'E was seen by two people climbin' down from my bedroom window an' when I went in the brooch 'ad gone. It was there before 'e went an' it wasn't there after 'e'd been. If 'e didn't take it, 'oo did?"

"He admits he took the penknife," said Mrs. Brown.

"If 'e took the penknife 'e took the brooch," said Mrs. Bott. "They was both there together an' they was both gone together. Tell me 'oo took them if 'e didn't, that's all."

"I don't know," said Mrs. Brown, "but I'm sure William didn't. I'm *quite* sure he didn't."

"An' I'm quite sure 'e did," said Mrs. Bott. "Well, that's all I've gotter say, Mrs. Brown. Either I gets back me brooch by the end of the week or I goes to the police. Take your choice. I'm bein' too lenient to the boy as it is. Shut up's what 'e oughter be, not goin' about robbin' people left an' right. E's à reg'lar young crim'nal an' he oughter be treated as such."

With that she turned on her heel and went away, leaving Mrs. Brown too stricken to reply.

William was amazed and horrified by the accusation. "I never *touched* her rotten ole brooch," he said. "It was there by the penknife an' I took the penknife but I left her rotten ole brooch. I remember seein' it by itself on the dressin' table. What should I want her rotten ole brooch for?"

"I really don't know, William," moaned Mrs. Brown. "I don't know what to do. Of *course* I know you didn't take it. Oh, I do wish your father were at home!"

For Mr. Brown had gone North on a business trip, and his wife did not know how to get in touch with him.

"It will be so dreadful for him to come home and find you in the hands of the police," she continued.

"But I didn't take it," repeated William. "I tell you, I *didn't* take it."

"I know you didn't, William," said Mrs. Brown, "but who's going to believe it when she tells a tale like that?"

"She's hid it herself jus' to pay me out for gettin' my penknife back," said William.

"No, William, I don't think she'd do that. . . . Oh dear, I do wish I knew what to do."

It was then that Joan arrived. She had arranged to play Red Indians with the Outlaws in the wood and had called for William on her way. William told her the story.

"Says I took her rotten old brooch," he said. "Makin' no end of a fuss about it. . . . Says she's goin' to the police if I don't give it her back by Saturday. Well, how can I when I've not got it?"

"Well, someone must have taken it," said Joan, "so what we've got to do is to find out who did take it."

"How can we do that?" said William. "They all say they found it gone after I'd been for my penknife."

"That horrible fortune teller woman took it," said Joan with calm certainty. "I *know* she did."

"Yes, I bet she did," said William with interest. "Yes, she looks 's if she'd do anythin'. But we can't prove she did."

"We must," said Joan. "*You* can't do anything 'cause they won't let you near the place now, but I can. I can try, anyway." She was silent for a few moments gazing thoughtfully into space, then said: "D'you remember when you used to go an' watch what that woman—I've forgotten her name—did every night an' then pretend you'd dreamed it 'cause you wanted her to think you could see things when you weren't there?"

"Yes, I remember," said William with a reminiscent chuckle.

"Well, I'm goin' to start that way," said Joan.

When Mrs. Bott was returning from the village the next morning she was accosted by a little girl whom she vaguely remembered to have recently come to live at Lilac Cottage—a little girl with a grave oval face, dark eyes and curly dark hair.

"Good afternoon, Mrs. Bott," said the little girl.

"Good afternoon, dear," said Mrs. Bott pleasantly. She disliked little boys, but on the whole she liked little girls. Violet Elizabeth, her own little girl, was away at boarding school, and, though she was not an amiable child, there were moments when her mother missed her.

The little girl began to walk with her down the country road.

"What's your name, dear?" said Mrs. Bott.

"Joan Parfitt," said Joan and, after a slight pause, "I had such a funny dream about you last night."

"Did you, dear?" said Mrs. Bott absently.

"Yes . . . I dreamed that you'd lost something very valuable and you were worrying about it . . . and you went to a sort of desk and wrote a letter to someone about it and then you sat down and did some needlework, and all the time you were worrying about the thing you'd lost. You were wearing a sort of purple dress. . . ."

Mrs. Bott stood stock still in the middle of the road and stared in amazement at the child who had dreamed exactly what she had been doing last night after dinner.

"Well, I never!" she gasped at last. "Well, I *never*! If that isn't the most *extraordinary* thing! Well, I never *did*!" Then, her voice sinking down to a solemn note: "I *was* doin' exactly that las' night, me dear. I wrote to a cousin telling 'er of this valuable thing I'd lost, then I did a bit of me tapestry work. 'Ow strange you should dream of it!"

Joan heaved a sigh of relief. The uncomfortable hour she had spent crouching outside Mrs. Bott's drawing-room window last night had not, then, been wasted.

"I often have dreams like that," she said modestly. "I often dream things that I find out afterwards are true."

"Well, if that doesn't—if that isn't——" gasped Mrs. Bott, still so deeply impressed she could not find words adequately to express her emotion. "Look 'ere, my dear, you didn't dream where this valu'ble thing was, did you?"

"No," admitted Joan, "I didn't. I didn't even know what it was. I got a feeling that it was something—small and shining, but that was all."

"Well, I'll be *blowed*!" gasped Mrs. Bott. "I've never known anythin' like it. Not in all me born days. It's—well, it's *wonderful*. Look 'ere, me dear. You come 'ome with me for a minute. I've someone at 'ome you mus' meet. She's got this Gift same as what you've got, an' she'll 'elp you develop it. Anyway, the three of us together oughter get physic enough to find out what that young villain's done with it. I know she'll be almost as int'rested as what I am to find you've got this gift. What a bit of luck—me meetin' you like this this mornin'!"

"Oh, you mean Madame Montpelimar," said Joan and added with well-simulated enthusiasm: "She's *wonderful*, isn't she?"

Mrs. Bott beamed down expansively at her companion. She had been piqued and disappointed by the failure of the village in general to appreciate her protégée. She had imagined that the Hall would become the centre of an extensive psychic movement with herself and Madame Montpelimar as its guiding spirits—and they had been shunned and ostracised. And yet here was this child—this gifted clairvoyante child—realising the greatness of her wonderful protégée, giving honour where honour was due. . . .

"Yes, she's a proper dab at it," said Mrs. Bott proudly. "She's learnin' me, too," she added. "She says I'm gettin' on a treat, but I've not been able to

MADAME MONTPELIMAR RECEIVED THE NEW RECRUIT
WITH RESERVE. SHE DIDN'T QUITE KNOW WHAT TO
MAKE OF HER.

find out where this 'ere brooch 'as gone to. You're
sure you didn't dream that, love?"

"Quite—but p'raps I'll dream that to-night," said
Joan shamelessly.

"Well, the first thing for you to do is to meet this 'ere Madame Montpelimar," said Mrs. Bott. "She'd 'elp you no end. An' she can explain dreams so you'll 'ardly recognise 'em."

Madame Montpelimar received the new recruit with reserve. She didn't quite know what to make of her, but decided in the end that, though one must, of course, keep an eye on her, she couldn't do much harm. Just a kid pulling old Ma Bott's leg. She used to do the same kind of thing when she was a kid, she remembered. Still did, come to that. . . .

In any case, Madame Montpelimar had troubles of her own and had no time to waste on other people's. The sprained ankle had turned out to be worse than it had seemed at first, and the doctor refused to allow her to leave the Hall. So there she was, tied by the leg with the goods still on her. However, she'd got out of tighter jams than that, and it was only a question of lying low till she could get away. The worst of it was that Mrs. Bott expected her to use her supposed clairvoyant gifts in order to discover the whereabouts of the brooch.

"I'm goin' to put the police on to that boy whether or no," she said grimly, "but I want to get my hands on that brooch. Wish I 'adn't given 'im a week now. 'E's prob'ly pawned it by now—or sold it. A young crim'nal like 'im knows where to get rid of the stuff all right. Prob'ly bin doin' it for years. . . . An' that there brooch meant a lot to me. Botty give it me for the first anniversary of our weddin'. Or maybe it was the second. I forget. Anyway, 'e'll take on something awful when he finds it's gone. . . . Can't you see what's 'appened to it, Madame Montpelimar? I mean, with your clairvoyance an' spirit voices an' dreams an' all. . . . I'd like to get it back before Botty comes."

And Madame Montpelimar made, to all appearances, every effort to discover the whereabouts of the missing brooch. She went into trances, she heard spirit voices, she dreamed dreams. But all to the same effect. She followed the course of the missing brooch from its resting-place on the dressing-table into the pocket of a boy's suit, followed it on its journey down a drain pipe, through a garden, down a road and into a house that, from her description, could be none other than the Browns' house. . . . And then, as she put it . . . "a cloud of evil seems to envelop me, Mrs. Bott—a real cloud of evil. I can see nothing more."

"Well, 'e's evil, all right," put in Mrs. Bott grimly. "I'll never forget the time 'e sent a stone clean through my tomato 'ouse. *An'* the time 'e let a mouse out in the Village 'All."

"So thick I can't see through it," went on Madame Montpelimar, ignoring the interruption. "Evil always has that effect on me. I'm over-sensitive to it. It paralyses my powers. . . ."

While deeply respecting this over-sensitiveness to evil on Madame Montpelimar's part, Mrs. Bott began to turn more and more to Joan, who continued to report "dreams" that faithfully reflected Mrs. Bott's actions of the evening before.

"I see you've got the Gift, love," said Mrs. Bott wistfully, "but I wish you would use it to find out where this brooch of mine's got to. I've tried myself all ways, but I can't get no dreams nor voices nor nothin'. I think I'm same as Madame Montpelimar—paralysed

by evil. She can see it right to this boy's house an'
then it all goes off into this 'ere cloud of evil. . . ."

And so Joan, who, in her determination to save
William, was discovering undreamed-of depths of
duplicity in herself, would describe dreams and feelings
in which she almost—but never quite—discovered the
whereabouts of the missing brooch.

"Well, you persevere, love," urged Mrs. Bott.
"There's no doubt you've got the Gift. Us physic ones
should hang together all we can, an' I'll be more grateful than I can say if you'll tell me where it is."

"I'll try again to-night," promised Joan.

Each day she took home a report to William.

"It's not in her bag. I said: 'What a nice bag!'
to-day and she let me take it and open it and try the
clasp. She wouldn't have done that if it had been in
it."

"It's not in her bedroom—I hunted everywhere
while they were having tea."

"It's not in false heels in her shoes. She's only got
two pairs and she lets them go into the kitchen to be
cleaned every day. She wouldn't do that if she'd put
it there. And her bedroom slippers are just felt
without heels at all."

"It's not anywhere in her clothes. She lets Mrs.
Bott's maid help her dress and undress. She wouldn't
do that if she was hiding it in her clothes."

"Well, where is it, then?" said William desperately.
"There's only one day now. P'raps," with rising
hopefulness, "ole Mrs. Bott'll forget about it."

"No, she isn't forgetting," said Joan. "She says
she's going to the police first thing to-morrow. She
keeps saying she's sorry she gave you that week."

"Gosh!" groaned William. "No one'll believe I didn't take it."

"Yes they *will*, William," said Joan. "There's a whole day left, and I'm sure to get an idea in a day."

That afternoon she went to the Hall as usual. Madame Montpelimar's sallow face wore a triumphant little smile. All danger now seemed over. The doctor had said that she could go home to-morrow. She intended to be well away, leaving no trace, before Mrs. Bott went to the police to lodge her accusation against William.

During the afternoon Joan happened to lean against the end of the sofa where Madame Montpelimar was reclining, and to touch the coils of coarse brown hair twisted round and round into the enormous "bun."

Madame Montpelimar moved her head sharply away.

"Mind Madame Montpelimar's head, Joan," said Mrs. Bott reverently. "It's very sensitive. It's on account of her astral body an' the spirit messages goin' in and out. She can't bear it touched. Won't even let Marie help her do it of a night and morning. Anyone but her touchin' it gives her agony, don't it, Madame Montpelimar?"

"It's been terribly sensitive ever since I was a child," admitted the clairvoyante, "ever since, in fact, the Gift first manifested itself in me."

Joan looked thoughtfully at Madame Montpelimar and still more thoughtfully at the bird's nest of coarse brown hair. Anything might be hidden in it. . . . But her dislike of the lady was tempered with respect, and she realised that even now she must go very carefully.

Finding Mrs. Bott alone in the morning-room a short time afterwards, she said:

MRS. BOTT SLIPPED A TABLET INTO THE LADY'S SECOND
CUP OF TEA.

"I've just remembered a sort of *message* I had last
night," she said.

Mrs. Bott looked at her, agog with excitement.

"A message, love?   A physic message?"

"Yes," said Joan.   "I heard it in a dream.   It

said that if Madame Montpelimar could go into a deep sleep directly after tea to-day—a *very* deep sleep—she'd dream where your brooch was. But she mustn't *know* she was going to or she wouldn't."

JOAN WAITED ASSIDUOUSLY ON MADAME MONTPELIMAR
AND DREW HER OUT TO TALK OF HER GIFT.

Mrs. Bott looked thoughtful.

"That's a bit awkward, love," she said. "She doesn't sleep after tea as a rule——"

"But I suppose she *could*," said Joan. "The doctor gave mother some things once when she couldn't sleep and she only used about two . . . I know where they are and I could get one."

"Oh, I've got some stuff meself," said Mrs. Bott. "Quite 'armless, the doctor said it was. . . . I don't see why. . . . Well, after all, she's as anxious to find that there brooch as any of us. . . . She'll be grateful when we tell 'er after it's all over."

Joan stayed to tea. She waited assiduously on Madame Montpelimar and drew her out to talk of her Gift, taking care to stand between her and the tea table while Mrs. Bott slipped a tablet into the lady's second cup of tea. Madame Montpelimar was in a genial expansive mood. This time to-morrow, she kept telling herself, I'll be safely off with the swag. . . .

She invented tall stories for Joan of futures she had foreseen, of catastrophes she had averted, of dreams and visions. . . . Irresistible languor began to steal over her.

"I feel a bit drowsy," she said. "I think I'll just put my feet up."

Joan and Mrs. Bott waited breathlessly as Madame Montpelimar put her feet up, rested her head on the cushions of the settee, closed her eyes and began to breathe deeply . . . more deeply. . . . .

Mrs. Bott came and stood by her.

"P'raps she's dreamin' where it is this very minute," she said in an awestruck voice.

Joan joined her.

"I don't think she looks very comfortable," she said, "and I don't think she can dream properly unless she's comfortable. I think her head would be much more comfortable if it hadn't all that hair to lie on. . . ."

"Better not touch her hair, love," said Mrs. Bott. "She never likes her hair touched."

But Joan was slowly and carefully taking out the hairpins. One long thick coil came down . . . another followed . . . another followed . . . and then, from the very centre of the erection, she took out something wrapped in brown silk and opened it before Mrs. Bott's incredulous gaze.

"It can't be," gasped Mrs. Bott. "It—it—it—it *can't* be."

But it was. . . .

And Madame Montpelimar—snoring slightly, blissfully unconscious—slept on. . . .

Madame Montpelimar—alias Princess Borinsky, alias Lady Vere Vereton, alias Baroness Gretchstein, alias Mary Smith—had been removed to the police station, where investigation was proving her to be a person whom the police had long wished to meet again. Mrs. Bott had been humbly, tearfully apologetic to William, offering him fantastic sums in compensation for the wrong she had done him—which Mrs. Brown, much to William's regret, firmly refused. Half a crown and permission to play in any part of the Hall grounds he wished, for an indefinite period, was finally considered to meet the needs of the case.

The next night William went to call for Joan.

"You did jolly well, Joan," he said.

"In a way I rather enjoyed it," said Joan.

"Well, I—I couldn't have done it better myself," said William, and it was a lot for William to admit. "Come on—let's spend the half-crown and then have that game of Red Indians."

CHAPTER V

RELUCTANT HEROES

"**D**'YOU know," said William thoughtfully at breakfast, "I don't seem to remember the time there wasn't a war."

"Don't be ridiculous, William," said his mother. "It's hardly lasted two years and you're eleven years old, so you must remember the time when there wasn't a war. All the same," she added with a sigh, "I know what you mean."

Certainly the war seemed to have altered life considerably for William. Sometimes he thought that the advantages and disadvantages cancelled each other out and sometimes he wasn't sure. . . . Gamekeepers had been called up and he could trespass in woods and fields with comparative impunity, but, on the other hand, sweets were scarce and cream buns unprocurable. Discipline was relaxed—at school as the result of a gradual infiltration of women teachers and at home because his father worked overtime at the office and his mother was 'managing' without a cook—but these advantages were offset by a lack of entertainment in general. There were no parties, summer holidays were out of the question because of something called the Income Tax, and for the same reason pocket money, inadequate at the best of times, had faded almost to vanishing point.

Now that Ethel was a V.A.D. and Robert a second lieutenant in one of the less famous regiments, home life had lost much of its friction, but it had also lost something of its zest. William had looked on Ethel and Robert as cruel and vindictive tyrants, but he found, somewhat to his surprise, that he missed both the tyranny and his own plans to circumvent and avenge it.

Even the feud with Hubert Lane lacked its old excitement. There didn't seem to be so many things to quarrel about as there had been before the war. Moreover, William needed a credulous audience for his tales of Robert's prowess and Hubert supplied it. For Robert, in his second lieutenant's uniform, was to William no longer an irascible dictatorial elder brother, hidebound by convention and deaf to the voice of reason. He was a noble and heroic figure, solely responsible for every success the British army had achieved since the war began. It was Robert who had conquered the Italians in Africa, raided the Lofoten Islands, crushed Raschid Ali's revolt. . . . Hubert was so credulous that William's stories grew more and more fantastic. It was Robert who, according to William, was solely responsible for the sinking of the *Bismarck*. It was Robert who had captured Rudolf Hess . . . But there even the worm of credulity that was Hubert turned.

"But Robert wasn't in Scotland when Rudolf Hess came over," he objected.

"How do you know he wasn't?" said William mysteriously. "Gosh! If I told you the places Robert had been in you wouldn't believe me."

"Well, there was nothing about him in the papers."

H

"No, they kept it out of the papers," said William. "Robert's very high up an' everythin' about him's gotter be kept very secret."

The worm of credulity turned still further.

"Thought he was only a second lieutenant."

William gave a short laugh.

"They keep him a second lieutenant just to put the Germans off the scent," he explained, "so they won't know who it is that's doing all these things."

"But I bet he didn't capture Rudolf Hess," persisted Hubert.

"Huh, didn't he!" said William, who was as usual now completely convinced by his own eloquence. "Well, I can't tell you about it 'cause it's a secret an' I'd get shot if I told people, but it was Robert got him over from Germany to start with."

"Crumbs!" gasped Hubert.

Hubert, however, though still, in the main, believing William's stories (as I have said, he was an exceptionally credulous boy), was growing a little tired of them. He'd listened to them for weeks on end and the one-sidedness of the situation was beginning to pall. If he'd had a few tales of his own to swop in exchange, he wouldn't have minded so much, but he hadn't. He was an only child and had no elder brother or even near relation to glorify. . . . Resentment had been slowly growing in his breast for some time, and the Rudolf Hess story seemed the last straw. He was not a boy to be content to yield the limelight to another indefinitely without becoming restive, and he was now becoming restive. He'd swallowed all Robert's exploits as recounted by William—the African victory, the defeat of Raschid Ali, the sinking of the *Bismarck*. . . .

"WHAT'S THE MATTER, HUBERT DEAR?" SAID HIS MOTHER
SOLICITOUSLY TO HIM AT LUNCH.

He had even swallowed Rudolf Hess, but—he'd reached saturation point.

"What's the matter, Hubert dear?" said his mother solicitously to him at lunch, looking at his plump, sulky face. "I hope you're not feeling ill, darling."

"No," muttered Hubert, "I'm not feelin' ill. I'm only sick of that ole William Brown."

Mrs. Lane shuddered at the name.

"I don't know why you have anything to do with him," she said. Then she turned to her husband. "Oh, by the way, I heard from Ronald this morning. He's got a week's leave and can spend it with us."

"Who's Ronald?" said Hubert.

"Didn't I tell you, dear? He's a second cousin of mine. We've never seen much of him because his people always lived in Switzerland. They're still there and so, of course, he can't spend his leave with them and will be very glad to spend it with us. . . . I asked him to bring a friend if he liked and he says he'd like to bring another lieutenant in his regiment, who has leave at the same time and has no relations in England to go to. It's rather amusing. He says"—she took a letter out of her pocket, opened it and read—"'I must warn you that Orford has the most amazing resemblance to Hitler. Actually he takes rather a pride in it, and cultivates the moustache and forelock. So don't think that I've brought Hitler back as a present when you see him.'"

Hubert put down his knife and fork and stared open-mouthed at his mother. He didn't often have ideas but he was having one now. It came slowly and painfully, and he turned paler than usual with the unaccustomed effort.

"Darling," cried Mrs. Lane in renewed concern, "you're not looking at *all* well. Don't you like the pudding?"

"No, I don't like the pudding," said Hubert calmly. "It's not sweet enough. But I'm feeling all right 'cept for that."

* * * * *

Hubert walked along the road with a new briskness. There was even a little smile on his face. He looked very pleased with himself. It happened that when he reached the gate of William's house, William himself was coming out of it. They went down the lane together.

"You know, when Robert captured the Hess man," began William, who had thought out a few more details during lunch, but Hubert interrupted him.

"Funny you should've told me that this morning," he said.

"Why?" said William.

"Well, it's jus' a sort of coincidence, that's all," said Hubert.

"What d'you mean, a coincidence?" said William, his curiosity aroused, as Hubert meant it to be.

"Will you promise not to tell anyone?" said Hubert.

"Yes."

"Cross your throat?"

"Cross my throat."

"Well, jus' the same sort of thing seems to've happened to a cousin of mine what's comin' to stay with us."

"The same sort of thing as what?" said William impatiently.

"Same sort of thing as Robert capturin' Hess."

"Dunno what you mean," said William. "Your

cousin couldn've captured Hess 'cause—I keep tellin'
you—Robert captured him."

"Oh no," said Hubert, "he's not captured Hess."
He paused a moment, then brought out with a superb
air of casualness: "He's captured Hitler."

"*What?*" gasped William, then, recovering himself,
said firmly: "He couldn't have."

"Why not?" said Hubert, who was enjoying a
conversation with William for the first time for weeks.

"'Cause he's not been captured."

"Oh yes, he has," said Hubert. "They've not put
it in the papers, of course, 'cause it's all gotter be kept
secret same as the things Robert does."

"Well——" William grappled helplessly with the
staggering idea. "Who's carryin' on in Germany
then?"

"One of his doubles," said Hubert. "He's got
dozens of 'em, you know."

William considered this, frowning thoughtfully.

"I bet this cousin of your mother's pullin' your leg,"
he said at last. "I bet he's not captured him really."

"Oh yes, he has," said Hubert confidently.

"Well, you've not got any proof," persisted William.
"He only *says* he's captured him. I bet he's pullin'
your leg."

Hubert was silent for a few moments, savouring his
triumph before he said, still with admirably acted
carelessness:

"Oh yes, I've got proof all right. He's bringin'
him here to-day."

"*What?*" squawked William. Then: "He *can't* be—
I *said* he was pullin' your leg."

"Yes, he is," said Hubert. "The gov'nment are

lettin' him keep him for a bit 'cause they want it kept secret that he's been captured. They don't want the Germans to know what's happened to him an' if they took him prisoner themselves they'd have to put it in the papers. So they're lettin' this cousin of mine keep him for a bit for his own prisoner. He's not dressed like he used to be," he added hastily. "He's disguised. He has to be, so's people won't recognise him."

"Has he got a false beard?" said William, to whom the story was beginning to seem as credible as Robert's exploits, recounted by himself.

"Oh no, he's not got a false beard," said Hubert. "That wouldn't be any good. They come off too easy, false beards. No, he's disguised as a British officer same as Robert or this cousin of mine. People'd never think it was Hitler, seein' him in an officer's uniform. An' he's gotter pretend he *is* a British officer, too, an' he's jolly glad to do it 'stead of bein' put in prison. This cousin of mine's taught him English, an' he talks it as well as you or me by now."

"Gosh!" said William. He took his seat on the top of a stile that led from the lane into a field. "Come on. Tell us all about it."

Hubert perched beside him and began the story that he had so carefully prepared on the way.

"Well, it was like this," he said. "This cousin of mine was walkin' out in the country one day an' he looked up an' saw a parachute comin' sailin' down from the sky. He ran up to where it landed an' saw it was ole Hitler, an' Hitler said he'd come over same as Hess 'cause ole Goering was after him, so this cousin of mine took him along an' rang up Churchill an' Churchill said: 'Well, let's have 'em on toast for a bit

wonderin' what's happened to him. Tell you what
—s'pose you keep him yourself 'cause if we take him
we'll have to put it in the papers. You'd better disguise him as an officer an' teach him English an' take
him about with you so's he can't escape.' So this
cousin of mine did an' when my mother wrote to ask
him to spend his leave with us he wrote back to say, yes,
he'd like to if he could bring ole Hitler along with him.''

Hubert paused, breathless and exhausted. It was
the greatest effort of imagination he had ever made
in his life. . . . William sat, elbows on knees, chin on
hands, gazing into space, considering the story.

"Bet this cousin of yours is pullin' your leg. Bet
he'll come alone an' have a good laugh at you for
believin' him.''

"All right," said Hubert. "He's comin' at six to-
night. You come along after that and have a look.''

"Yes, I jolly well will," said William.

Hubert walked home happily. He had enjoyed the
afternoon more than he had enjoyed any afternoon
since the war began. It had been a refreshing change
to hold forth to William instead of being held forth to
by William. It had been a triumph to have concen-
trated the limelight upon himself instead of watching
William enjoy it. It should be quite easy to sustain
the Hitler fiction for the few days of his cousin's visit.
Fortunately his mother cherished a deep dislike of
William as a "nasty rough boy" and had long ago
forbidden him the house.

The excitement with which William had first heard
the news decreased slightly as he walked homeward.
The cousin had been pulling ole Hubert's leg, of course.
Anyone could pull ole Hubert's leg. He'd done it

himself dozens of times. He would go round there after tea and he'd bet anyone anything he'd just find ole Hubert's cousin having a good laugh at him.

He waited impatiently till six o'clock, then set off towards the Lanes' house. Not wishing to risk an encounter with Mrs. Lane, he concealed himself behind the hedge in a position that gave him a good view of the garden. The garden was empty. No one could be seen at any of the windows of the house.

"Bet the whole thing's a leg-pull," muttered William. "Bet he hasn't even got a cousin comin' to stay at all."

Then the side door opened, and out came Hubert, Mrs. Lane and a tall fair man in uniform.

"Hasn't brought a friend at all," said William. "Pullin' ole Hubert's leg. I said he was all the time. It's a jolly good joke. I'll have a jolly good laugh at him to-morrow. I'll have a jolly good . . ." His mouth dropped open. His eyes goggled. For at the side door appeared a figure long familiar to him from photographs and caricatures. It was bareheaded. The short moustache, the dark lank forelock, the pallid morose face. . . .

"Gosh!" gasped William, going suddenly weak at the knees. "*Gosh!* It's him!"

And, without stopping to consider anything further, he turned to flee as if the whole of the Gestapo were at his heels.

"What on earth's the matter, William?" said his mother as he flung himself, panting and dishevelled, into the house a few minutes later, turning to bolt and bar the front door. "What *are* you doing that for?"

William gazed at her, still panting. He longed to tell her the whole story, but he had never yet broken a "cross my throat" promise and he wasn't going to start now. Besides, on thinking the matter over, he decided that there wasn't really anything to be afraid of. The prisoner was safely in his captor's hands. Hubert's cousin was presumably armed and would not allow him to escape.

"Nothin'," he said. "Well, nothin' *you* need worry about. He wouldn't dare start any of his tricks over here."

"What *are* you talking about, William?"

"Nothin'," said William, drawing back the bolt. "I

WILLIAM'S MOUTH DROPPED OPEN. HIS EYES GOGGLED.

bet we'll be all right. I've got my bow an' arrows, anyway, if he does start any tricks."

He shadowed the illustrious captive from a respectful

FOR AT THE SIDE DOOR APPEARED A FIGURE LONG
FAMILIAR TO HIM.

distance all the next day. The illustrious captive went for a walk with Hubert's cousin in the morning and stayed in the garden in the afternoon. William overheard him commenting on the countryside in excellent English. Certainly Hubert's cousin had done that part of the job successfully. As Hubert had said, he spoke English as well as—or indeed better than—Hubert and William themselves.

The next day the two of them went up to London, and William spent the day in Hubert's company listening to repeated accounts of the capture. Hubert was not gifted with any great imaginative powers and, having with an almost superhuman effort invented the story of the capture, he saw no reason to alter or add to it. William did not exactly become bored—one could hardly be bored by such a story—but he wanted a few more details.

"Well, what's he goin' to do with him next?" he asked.

"Oh, he's just gotter wait till Mr. Churchill tells him what to do."

"Hasn't ole Hitler ever tried to get away?"

"No, he knows he couldn't get away," said Hubert. "This cousin of mine'd shoot him soon as look at him if he tried gettin' away."

"Does he lock him in his room at night or sleep chained to him or what?"

"No," said Hubert, "he knows he won't try to get away."

Despite the undeniable excitement of the situation, there seemed something too static about it for William's taste. It was so fraught with drama that drama should, as it were, spring from it continually.

"Wish he'd try to escape," he said. "I bet I'd catch

him if he did.   He'd be my prisoner then, wouldn't he?"

"Dunno," said Hubert vaguely, "but anyway, he won't try.   He knows he couldn't get back to Germany an' he quite likes my cousin.   He says he reminds him of Gobbles."

"He's not a bit like Gobbles," objected William.

"Well, it may be one of the others," said Hubert, who was finding the whole thing, though enjoyable, something of a tax on his intellect.   "It may be Himmler or Mussolini or someone.   Anyway, he says he reminds him of someone.   P'raps it was his father . . . I say, you've not told anyone, have you?   My cousin'd get in an awful row with Mr. Churchill if you've told anyone."

"'Course I haven't," said William indignantly.   "I said 'cross my throat', di'n't I?"

But the keeping of the secret was not proving easy. It hovered on the tip of William's tongue a hundred times a day, though he always managed to choke it back.   He decided at last that it could do no harm to hint at the possession of a piece of extraordinary knowledge. . . .

"I bet I know somethin' that'd give you a shock if you knew about it, Mother," he said portentously as he entered the morning-room.

But Mrs. Brown had an exciting piece of information of her own to impart.

"I've had a wire to-day, William," she said. "Robert's coming home on leave."

And that, for the moment, drove the thought of the secret right out of William's head.   Robert, the hero, who had conquered Africa, sunk the *Bismarck* and

WILLIAM MEANT ROBERT TO BE A HERO, THEREFORE
ROBERT MUST BE A HERO.

crushed Raschid Ali's revolt . . . William's soul
thrilled at the thought of meeting him again.

When Robert actually arrived, however, William
found it a little difficult to sustain this attitude.
Robert in uniform was so devastatingly like Robert
out of uniform—an irascible unreasonable elder brother,
passionately interested in such trivial affairs as football
results, the fit of his tunic, and the girl friend of the
moment. It became more and more difficult to reconcile him with the hero of the sagas that William had so
assiduously woven around him. It wasn't easy even
to imagine his capturing Hess. . . . But William, born
hero-worshipper, was determined to see Robert as he
wished to see him. He meant Robert to be a hero,

therefore Robert must be a hero. It would have been easier to reconcile oneself to the old unheroic Robert had it not been for Hubert's cousin with his glorious prize just across the way. The more William thought of this, the more intolerable seemed the state of affairs. He would not submit to it. Robert was a hero. Robert should be a hero. Robert *must* be a hero.... And yet the situation didn't seem to be one that admitted of heroism. There were not likely to be any more Nazi leaders drifting in parachutes from the skies. It was a pity, thought William regretfully, that Robert had not been there instead of Hubert's cousin when Hitler came down. And then—quite suddenly—William had his idea. It was a stupendous idea. Robert had not captured Hitler, but he could still capture him. There was Hitler under his very nose only about a quarter of a mile away. He could capture him from Hubert's cousin and then he would be his—Robert's—captive, until such time as the government saw fit to claim him as their own. William, of course, still considered himself bound by his promise. He could not tell Robert in so many words that the Fuehrer was a prisoner at the Lanes' house and ripe for recapture, but he could surely induce the captive to attempt escape and then put Robert on his track. That, though sailing a bit near the wind, wouldn't, he considered, be actually breaking his promise. The scheme called for careful planning. The first thing to do was to get Hitler by himself, and that wouldn't be easy because naturally he spent most of his time in company with his captor.

It was only after a whole day's continuous stalking that William managed to secure his prey. He came upon Lieutenant Orford walking back alone from the village. Rather apprehensively—for, after all, this was the man who murdered friends and enemies alike by thousands in cold blood, and it was a lonely stretch of road—William sidled up to him.

"I say," he said in a conspiratorial whisper, "why don't you run away?"

Lieutenant Orford stared at him in surprise.

"What on earth are you talking about?" he said.

"There's no one about," said William. "I bet you could run away all right."

Lieutenant Orford waved him impatiently aside and strode on down the road without answering.

William gazed after him regretfully. *That* hadn't been any good. Evidently he didn't want to run away. Scared of being shot, probably. . . . He must try to think of some more cunning plan. . . . Suddenly he thought of one. He ran to catch up the swiftly moving figure.

"I say!" he panted. "Hubert's cousin sent a message for you."

The swiftly striding figure stopped. "Why on earth couldn't you have said that before?" he snapped.

"Were you expecting a message?" said William cunningly.

"'Course I was," snapped Lieutenant Orford. "He said that if he'd started before I got back he'd leave a message where he'd gone to."

"Oh," said William. "Well, he's started. He's gone to"—he summoned all his inventive powers—"he's gone to Poppleham. D'you know where that is?"

"Never heard of it," said Lieutenant Orford.

"Well, he told me to take you to it if you didn't know

it," said William. "I don't s'pose you know England very well, do you?"

Lieutenant Orford ignored this remark and they walked on in silence for some moments. Then William said casually:

"I expect you liked it in Germany, di'n't you?"

"Liked what?" said Lieutenant Orford shortly.

"Well, you know, liked it," said William vaguely, and added after a short pause: "What d'you think of Hess?"

"I don't think about him at all," said Lieutenant Orford.

Again conversation flagged. William led his companion over a stile and across a field, breaking the silence finally with: "I expect they're wonderin' what's happened to you over there."

"Who?" snapped Lieutenant Orford, "and over where?"

William sighed. The illustrious captive was evidently determined not to give himself away. Probably he'd made a "cross my throat" promise not to.

"Oh well," he said, "I suppose you don't want people to know about it."

"Where *is* this Poppleham place?" said Lieutenant Orford irritably.

He was tired of trailing over the countryside with a half-witted child.

"We're nearly there," said William.

They had reached the old barn now and the next thing was to lure his captive into it.

"I say!" he said, pausing at the open door and peering into the dark corner. "There's somethin' funny in that corner, isn't there?"

Lieutenant Orford was not devoid of curiosity. He stepped into the barn. William pushed the door to and shot home the bolt.

*   *   *   *   *

Robert, seated comfortably in a deck-chair in the garden, looked up at William with a mixture of helplessness and elder-brother severity.

"I don't know *what* you're talking about," he said shortly.

"Well, I keep *tellin'* you," persisted William. "This man came down in a parachute an' he was dressed like a British officer an' he asked me in German where Rudolph Hess was an'——"

"You don't know any German," objected Robert.

"No, but he translated it into broken English for me an' I got him to the ole barn an' locked him in. He looked to me sort of as if he might be Hitler, an' I thought it'd be nice for you to take him prisoner."

"Don't be ridiculous," said Robert. "He couldn't *possibly* be Hitler."

"All right," shrugged William, "but he'd got a face like Hitler's an' he came down by a parachute in a British uniform an' started talkin' German."

"Was it a khaki uniform?"

"Yes."

"Where's the parachute?"

"Dunno. Think he must have hid it."

"It's a ridiculous story," said Robert again, pretending to return to his book.

It sounded ridiculous, of course, but Robert wasn't quite happy about it. Ridiculous things of that sort had happened all over Europe and might happen in England any day, impossible as it still seemed. Sup-

pose there were something in the kid's tale, after all. ...
It wouldn't do any harm to verify it. He stood up
and closed his book.

"I happen to be going in that direction," he said
loftily. "You can come along if you like."

*　　*　　*　　*　　*

Lieutenant Orford had spent a very uncomfortable
quarter of an hour trying to escape from the old barn.
It had no windows and, though the door was old, it
held firmly. He had kicked and shouted, but no one
had heard him. His anger against the half-witted
child, who had locked him in had risen to boiling point
when suddenly the door opened, revealing the half-
witted child in company with a young man. Without
stopping to consider, Lieutenant Orford leapt forward
to execute vengeance. Robert, for his part, had taken
for granted that the whole story was one of William's
fantastic inventions. When therefore a figure in khaki,
with what in the semi-darkness looked like the face of
the German Fuehrer in one of his brain-storms, hurled
itself upon them, he lost no time in closing with it.
They fought fiercely and silently. Though they were
fairly well matched, Robert seemed to be getting the
best of it.

"Hold on, Robert!" shouted William. "I'll go and
get a rope."

It had occurred to him suddenly that it would be a
fine score over Hubert if Robert could lead his prisoner
past the Lanes' house at the end of a rope. ...

*　　*　　*　　*　　*

William sat in the wheelbarrow, munching an apple
and gazing morosely at the next door cat, who sat on
the fence that divided the gardens, gazing morosely

"HOLD ON, ROBERT!" SHOUTED WILLIAM. "I'LL GO
AND GET A ROPE."

back at William. The adventure had ignominiously
petered out to nothing. To worse than nothing . . .
for Robert, from being super-hero, had become again
the old Robert, unheroic but with a swift sure hand for

avenging insults and injuries, and he had considered that the events of the afternoon constituted both. . . .

It had taken William some time to secure a rope and when he returned to the old barn he had found it empty. He had scoured the countryside for traces of either Robert or his captive, and had then returned home to find the two of them in amicable converse in the morning-room. The visitor had a black eye and Robert a swollen nose. Robert fell upon William without ceremony and it was the visitor who finally rescued him.

"Let the kid off now," he said. "It wasn't a bad joke and I thoroughly enjoyed the scrap. It's years since I had a really good one. You're pretty useful with your left, you know."

"My defence is too slow," said Robert modestly. "You were too quick for me. But it was a jolly good scrap."

It turned out that Robert and Lieutenant Orford had taken to each other. Lieutenant Orford was bored to death with Hubert's cousin and the Lanes. He and Robert were fixing up various dates for the remainder of their leave. They wouldn't even listen to William when he tried to explain what had happened.

"Get *out*!" ordered Robert threateningly.

And William got out.

He munched his apple, continuing to stare morosely at the next door cat. The next door cat had, as he knew, troubles of its own. From a diet of sardines, chicken and cream, it had gradually been relegated to skim milk and a nauseous bran-like mixture sold under the misleading name of Cat Food. Meeting William's eye, it opened its mouth in a raven-like croak of disgust.

"Huh!" said William through a mouthful of apple. "It's all right for *you*.   *You've* not had your leg pulled by Hubert Lane."

The cat eyed him sardonically and repeated its raven-like croak.

"An' been half killed on top of it," continued William. "Gosh! I'm sorry for those Germans when Robert gets at 'em."

He aimed his apple core at the cat.   It missed it by several feet.

"Can't even hit a cat," he continued dejectedly.

The cat uttered what sounded like a sardonic chuckle.

William sank back again into the wheelbarrow and took another apple out of his pocket.

"You're right," he agreed as he bit into it.   "It's a rotten war."

CHAPTER VI

GUY FAWKES—WITH VARIATIONS

"GUY FAWKES' day without a bonfire or fire-works!" said William despondently. "It's not right. It oughter be put a stop to."

"I've almost forgot what a firework looks like," said Ginger.

"It seems wrong to a great man like that," said Douglas in a tone of righteous indignation, "lettin' people forget him jus' 'cause of the war."

"He wasn't a great man," Henry reminded him. "He tried to blow up the Houses of Parliament."

"Well, that's where the Gov'nment lives, isn't it?" said Douglas, "an' to hear my father talk when his Income Tax comes in you'd think it was a good thing if someone did blow it up."

"Well, it's against the lor, anyway," persisted Henry. "There's lors stoppin' people blowin' up the Gov'nment."

"It doesn't matter what sort of man he was," said William impatiently. "We can't have fireworks or a bonfire an' it's jolly rotten."

"He must've done somethin' else besides try to blow up the Gov'nment," said Ginger.

"He didn't," said Henry. "That's all he ever did an' he got executed for it."

William thought this over in silence, then brightened.

"Well, if we can't have him blowin' up the Gov'nment we can have him bein' executed," he suggested.

The others considered the suggestion with various degrees of doubtfulness.

"How can we?" demanded Douglas.

"Well, don't you see?" said William, "it's quite easy. One of us'll be Guy Fawkes—I'll be him—an' we can act him blowin' up the Gov'nment—one of you can be the Gov'nment—an' then another can be the policeman an' another the judge. An' we can have a trial an' an execution. I'll be the executioner. I'll borrow our axe from the tool-shed."

"You can't if you're Guy Fawkes," said Ginger. "You couldn't chop your own head off."

"N-no," agreed William, reluctantly abandoning this double role. "No, I s'pose I couldn't. Least, I bet I could, but it'd take a lot of practice. All right, the p'liceman can cut his head off.... Anyway, it's better than nothin'. It's not as good as a bonfire, but it's better than jus' doin' nothing. Well, it's better than a bonfire in one way 'cause it won't matter if it rains."

The others were gradually becoming infected by William's enthusiasm.

"The old barn can be the Houses of Parliament," said Ginger. "An' I'm bein' the Gov'nment in it."

"I'll come an' blow you up soon as you've got settled," said William. "I bet I can get somethin' that goes off with a bang. An' then I'll run away an' Douglas'll be the p'liceman an' run after me."

"Bet I catch you!" cried Douglas exultantly.

"An' I'm the judge," said Henry. "I'll have witnesses an' speeches an' things same as a real one."

"Then I chop your head off," said Ginger with relish.

"Bet you don't," said William. "Bet I escape out of prison."

"You can't do things the real one didn't," said Henry.

"Can't I!" said William. "You wait an' see!"

The game undoubtedly promised a certain amount of surprise and excitement.

"It's not till to-morrow," said Ginger. "It gives us time to think out lots of extra things to put into it."

"Yes," said William, "we'll all think hard till to-morrow."

It was on the way home that they met Joan, wandering somewhat disconsolately down the lane.

"Hello, Joan," said William. "We're havin' Guy Fawkes' day to-morrow without a bonfire. Would you like to be in it? You can't be Guy Fawkes," hastily, "because I'm him."

"Nor the Gov'nment nor executioner," said Ginger, "'cause I'm them."

"Nor the p'liceman," said Douglas, "'cause I'm him."

"Nor the judge," said Henry.

"Can I be his mother?" said Joan.

"He didn't have a mother," said William.

"He must have done," put in Henry.

"Well, I mean she didn't come into it," explained William. "She didn't blow anything up."

Joan considered.

"Did he have a wife? Did she do anything?"

The Outlaws looked nonplussed.

"*Someone* in history had a wife," volunteered Ginger, "an' she went to see him in prison an' changed clothes with him an' he went out in her clothes an' got away."

"I don't think it was Guy Fawkes," said Henry.

"Don't see why it shouldn't've been," said William. "It'd make it a bit more excitin', anyway. It takes a jolly lot of other excitin' things to make up for a bonfire."

"I'll be Mrs. Fawkes, then," said Joan, "and I'll come and see you in prison and you can come out in my coat and hat. The hat comes right down over my face so it'll make a good disguise." She sighed. "I shall be glad to have something to do to-morrow. It's going to be an *awful* day."

"Why?" chorused the Outlaws.

She began to walk down the road with them.

"Well, it's a cousin of Mummy's. I've never seen her, but she's got a school in a terribly safe place in Scotland, and she says she'll take me as a pupil without Mummy paying anything, and Mummy says that with things being so difficult because of the war we oughtn't to say 'no'. I don't want to go and Mummy doesn't really want me to go, but she says we mustn't refuse 'cause it's such an opportunity with it being such a good school and such a terribly safe place, but—oh, I can't bear to *think* of it. . . ."

"You're not goin' to-morrow, are you?" said William, aghast.

He had begun to take Joan's presence for granted, and the thought of her sudden disappearance from their games and expeditions was a disconcerting one. Joan was quiet and unobtrusive, but she filled a distinct need in their lives. She played squaw to their Red Indians (and no one had ever made a better squaw), and looked

"I'LL BE MRS. FAWKES, THEN," SAID JOAN, "AND I'LL
COME AND SEE YOU IN PRISON."

after them generally, concealing the trails of untidiness
and destructiveness they left behind them, brushing
coats and straightening collars before they returned
to the keen maternal eye. She was, in short, both
officially and unofficially their Squaw-in-Chief.

"No, not to-morrow," she said mournfully. "I'm
going there next term probably, but this cousin—she's
called Miss Cummins—is coming over to see my mother
about it to-morrow, and to get it all fixed up. I was
just *dreading* to-morrow, but if I can be Mrs. Fawkes
it'll be *one* thing to look forward to, anyway, and it
won't be quite so bad."

"But—*gosh*!" protested William indignantly, "you
can't go to this place. Why, it's—it's—it's *safe* all
right here."

"Not so safe as in this terribly safe place where she
has her school," said Joan sorrowfully, "and Mummy
says it'll be nice for Daddy not having to pay any more
school fees for me. She doesn't *want* me to go. She's
as miserable as I am about it—but she thinks we *ought*
to."

"Well, I think it's rotten," said William.

The other Outlaws agreed.

"Never mind," said Joan brightening. "Let's forget it. It's lovely to have the Guy Fawkes thing to
look forward to. I think it'll be much nicer than a
bonfire. Let's all be conspirators to start with and
then we can be the other parts afterwards. It'll be
more fun to have a lot of conspirators. What are you
going to blow it up with, William? I've got some
pistol caps."

"Oh, good!" said William. "We've used everything
up like that, an' you can't get 'em now."

They walked down the road, discussing the details of the Guy Fawkes' day celebrations.

*   *   *   *   *

The conspirators met at the appointed place—under an oak tree near the old barn. They all wore mackintoshes as being the nearest approach to conspirators' cloaks that could be produced, and threw furtive glances over their shoulders as they talked. All of them had luxuriant corked moustaches.

"What'll we do to get rid of the Gov'nment?" said Ginger, and added "Gadzooks!" with an air of conscious erudition.

"Methinks 'twere best to poison it," suggested Henry. "Put arsenic in its tea same as I once read about a man doin' in the newspaper."

"Marry, no," said Henry in a deep bass voice, adding in his natural voice: "Marry's another of 'em, same as Gadzooks." He returned to his deep bass voice. "Let's hide behind a hedge anon an' shoot it. Anon's another," he added in parenthesis.

"Nay, marry anon gadzooks!" said William, rather overdoing it. "We might miss it. Then we'd all get shot. I tell thee what! Let's blow it up."

"Nay, sirrah," said Henry, "'twould be a jolly dangerous thing to do. I bet thee anything they'd find out."

"Hearken unto me," began Joan.

"That's too Bible," interrupted Henry. "He's not out of the Bible, Guy Fawkes. He's out of history."

"What shall I say, then?" said Joan.

"Oh, you could jus' say 'List' an' put 'Gadzooks' in front."

"All right," said Joan. "Gadzooks, list." She

thought for a moment, then said: "What about gramercy? Isn't that one too?"

"Yes," said Henry vaguely, "I believe it is."

"What do they mean, anyway?" said Ginger.

"Nothin'," said Henry. "They jus' stuck 'em about anywhere to show they were talkin' history language."

"All right," said Joan. "List, marry anon gramercy. Why should'st we not dig a sort of tunnel from next door to the Houses of Parliament and blow them up that way? They did that really."

"And a jolly good way anon," said William.

"I don't think 'anon's' right," said Henry. "I think 'anon' means something."

"No, I think it's jus' a history word," said William, "an' we want a good many with so many of us. Come on, my merry men——"

"That's Robin Hood," criticised Henry. "It's outlaws that's merry men, not conspirators."

"Y-yes, I suppose so," agreed William. "All right. Come on——"

"Varlet!" said Henry excitedly. "I've jus' remembered. They called people varlets in hist'ry."

"All right," said William. "Come on, my ole varlets. Let us haste with all speed, gadzooks, to do the gunpowder plot."

The next scene was simpler. William, Joan, Douglas and Henry, still wearing mackintoshes, made furtive and conspiratorial play of digging a tunnel outside the old barn, while, inside, Ginger, impersonating the Government, sat on a packing-case, sucking a stout twig, intended to represent a cigar. At the appropriate moment Douglas detached himself from the conspira-

tors and reappeared as the policeman, wearing his
mother's enamel cullender as a helmet. A spirited
fight ensued, in the course of which William was secured
and dragged to the old barn as a prisoner. The trial
that followed was, in effect, little more than a continua-
tion of the fight, ending in single combat between judge
and accused. Finally William was shut up in the old
barn, with Ginger, Henry and Douglas on guard outside.

Joan approached with small mincing steps. She
wore her green coat and hat, the hat pulled well over
her eyes.

A SPIRITED FIGHT ENSUED, IN THE COURSE OF WHICH
WILLIAM WAS SECURED AS A PRISONER.

"Good afternoon, varlets," she said in a high-pitched affected voice. "I am Mrs. Fawkes. Prithee let me see my husband. 'Tis visiting day, and I have come to see him."

"You've gotter bribe us," said Ginger. "They always bribed people in history."

"All right," said Joan. "I'll give thee three bulls' eyes each when I get my next pocket-money on Saturday."

"Bet you won't get any bulls' eyes," said Ginger. "I couldn't get any las' Sat'day when I tried. They'd only got some beastly little cough lozenges that the taste of made you feel sick."

"They've got some lollipops in Hadley," said Douglas.

"Yes," said Henry bitterly, "but they're so small you can hardly see 'em. I bought one an' it all sucked away to nothin' before I could taste it."

"Milk chocolate!" said Joan in a far-away voice. "Jus' think of the slabs an' *slabs* you used to get before the war."

"*Here!*" shouted the prisoner indignantly from inside the prison. "Get *on* with it, can't you? Don't stand out there all day jabberin' about *sweets!*"

Thus recalled to their roles, the actors harshly reassumed their parts.

"All right, then," said Ginger gruffly to Joan. "Ye canst go in and have a look at him. Don't stay for long or thou'll get thine head cut off."

"Say 'Gadzooks'," prompted William from inside. "You're forgettin' to talk hist'ry."

"I'm sick of all those words that don't mean anythin'," said Ginger. "I'm not goin' to say 'em any more."

"Hie me!" said Henry with a fresh burst of excitement. "They said 'Hie me' instead of 'go'. I've just remembered. I read it somewhere." He turned to Joan. "All right. Hie thee to thy husband."

"Thanks awfully," said Joan. "I won't be long and I won't forget the bulls' eyes. All right," in answer to a fresh burst of impatience from the prisoner. "I'm just hiemeing, William—I mean Guy."

* * * * *

Mrs. Parfitt gazed despairingly at the visitor across the tea-table. She had not met her cousin (actually it was a somewhat complicated relationship of the "twice removed" kind) since childhood, and she remembered her as one of those obedient, tidy, punctual children who never tear their clothes or lose their tempers and are held up as models to all other children for miles around.

She found that she had changed very little. She was still self-satisfied and opinionated and devastatingly efficient.

She took the cup of tea that Mrs. Parfitt handed her and nibbled a Shrewsbury cake. Her very nibble had something smug about it.

"I look upon this as my war work," she said. "I said to myself: 'I will educate free some child who has a claim on me and whose parents have suffered as the result of the war.' And of course, my thoughts went first to your little girl. She is definitely a connection, and your husband's business has suffered as the result of the war, has it not?"

"It has indeed," sighed Mrs. Parfitt. "His London warehouse was bombed, you know."

"Joan, then, will be fed and lodged and taught with

K

no expense to you at all," said Miss Cummins. "My school has a good standing in the educational world, and the locality in which it is situated has never even heard the alert. I have many members of the aristocracy as pupils in the school. Joan is, in fact," she ended in a glow of self-approval, "an extremely lucky child."

"Yes, of course she is," said Mrs. Parfitt with growing dismay. "We shall miss each other terribly, of course. . . ."

"That shows what an excellent thing it is for you both," breezed Miss Cummins. "It is my belief that a child cannot be rescued—*rescued*, I say—too soon from the bonds of the parent's possessive love. In my school Joan will be taught to stand on her own feet. Her character will be moulded to the pattern that I have set as the ideal of all my pupils. I should prefer to keep her with me during the holidays—I generally find home influence so demoralising for children—but I suppose you will not agree to that."

"Oh *no*," pleaded Mrs. Parfitt. "I *must* have her for holidays."

"I will waive that point for the present, then," said Miss Cummins graciously. "I shall expect Joan, of course, to work hard and to do everything she can to help me personally in order to show her gratitude. She must remember that the parents of the other children pay fees amounting to over two hundred pounds a year. I don't mean, of course, that Joan will be treated in any way differently from the others, but it is a wonderful chance for her and she should realise it." She glanced at her watch. "I ought to go to catch my train now. I'd hoped for a word with Joan herself."

"I didn't know you'd have to go so early," said Mrs.

Parfitt. "She's out playing with her friends. They generally play somewhere near that old barn you see from the road. I'll come to the station with you and perhaps we'll see her on the way."

"No, no," said Miss Cummins imperiously. "I prefer to speak to the child alone. No child is perfectly natural in the presence of its parents. I would not, of course, say this to everyone, but the influence of a normal parent upon a normal child is one that definitely retards the development. I will go myself to the station and hope to meet Joan on the way. I've never seen her, have I?"

"No," said Mrs. Parfitt, "but she's wearing a green coat and hat. You can't mistake her. . . . It's the only one in the neighbourhood. Of course, they may have gone into the woods."

"Then I'll just take my chance and hope for the best," said Miss Cummins. "Good-bye. So nice to have seen you again after all these years. I find you have changed very little, and I hope you can say the same of me. You may leave Joan in my charge with a clear mind. She will have every possible advantage. I strive to implant in my pupils those qualities that I have always striven to attain myself."

She walked briskly down the path to the road.

Mrs. Parfitt watched her out of sight, then turned to the handsomely bound school prospectus that Miss Cummins had left and stood absently turning over the pages. It was an imposing prospectus, showing spacious classrooms and palatial assembly hall, swimming-bath and acres of beautifully tended grounds . . . but Mrs. Parfitt looked at it with singularly little pleasure.

* * * * *

William, wearing Joan's coat and hat—the hat pulled
well down over his eyes—came out of the old barn and
addressed the guards outside in a high-pitched squeaky
voice.

"Thank thee, varlets," he said, "for letting me visit

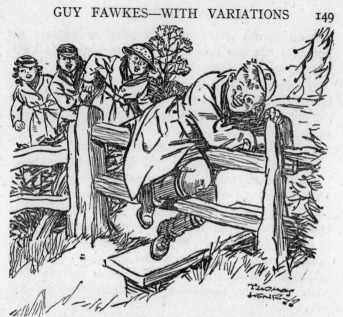

AT THIS POINT A CROWD OF CHILDREN APPEARED.
MISS CUMMINS' COMPANION GAVE AN EAR-SPLITTING
YELL AND TORE DOWN THE FIELD.

my husband, Mr. Guy Fawkes. I won't forget the
bulls' eyes on Saturday. Good afternoon," and hurried away across the field down towards the road.

In order to make the situation more exciting, the
guards had agreed to wait about five minutes before
discovering the "trick" played on them. This would
give William time to escape and afford an opportunity
for a hunt over the countryside.

William had decided to make for the woods, where
he knew of several good hiding-places. He had entered
fully into his role and saw himself as Guy Fawkes,

dressed in his wife's clothes, bent on eluding his pursuers. It was annoying to run straight into a tall woman walking down the road.

She gazed at him through horn-rimmed spectacles. Miss Cummins had noticed the old barn and had seen the figure in green coat and hat leave it to hurry across the field.

"It's Joan, isn't it?" she said tentatively.

"Uh-huh," said William, looking up at her.

Miss Cummins started. As head mistress of a large girls' school she was familiar with various degrees of plainness in her pupils, but she thought she had never come across such an uncompromisingly ugly little girl in all her life before. And not only ugly—but hard, brazen, tough. Yes, tough was the word. A tough little girl. Miss Cummins shuddered at the combination. Scowling aggressively, William returned her gaze.

"D'you want anything?" he said impolitely.

"Are you Joan Parfitt?" said Miss Cummins.

"Yeah," said William, determined to sustain his disguise. How did he know who the woman was? A spy probably. Ginger's family had a schoolmistress billeted on them, whom William had not seen yet and who, Ginger said, was one of those sickening people who were always trying to "enter into the children's games." Ginger had said yesterday that he had with difficulty stopped her coming with him to play Red Indians in the wood. For all he, William, knew, she had found out about this game and was "entering into it," pretending to be a detective. . . .

Miss Cummins glanced with increasing disapproval at the short stocky figure. The stubby wiry hair beneath the green hat was cropped short like a boy's. The child was evidently wearing a battered pair of boy's shorts. Her knees were filthy, her stockings rumpled, and she wore a pair of stout clumsy hob-nailed shoes. Odd, because her green coat and hat were well-tailored, though the child had obviously outgrown them. The child, of course, could not help her looks, but her manners seemed to be as ungainly as her appearance. It would certainly be one of the hardest cases her school had ever tackled. . . .

"And where are you off to?" said Miss Cummins.

William's suspicion that the unknown was Ginger's family's evacuee "butting into the game" deepened. He decided to nip it in the bud.

"You mind your own business," he said brusquely.

Miss Cummins blenched. Never in all her life had a child spoken to her like that before.

"You'll have to learn to be more polite than that if you come to my school," she said grimly.

"I'm not coming to your rotten ole school," said William.

At this point a crowd of children suddenly appeared, tearing down the field, tumbling over the stile, obviously in pursuit of Miss Cummins' companion.

Miss Cummins' companion gave an ear-splitting yell and tore off down the road, followed by the others. In a few moments the whole pack—all uttering ear-splitting yells—had plunged across another field, into a wood . . . and peace descended once more upon the countryside.

Miss Cummins continued her progress towards the railway station. She didn't remember feeling so shaken since the time a visiting lecturer had deliberately introduced Socialism into a lecture on Economics. Her nerves were a-jangle, her head aching from the ear-splitting yells.

"No," she said with a little shudder. "I couldn't bear it. War work or no war work, I simply couldn't bear it."

*   *   *   *   *

Joan and her mother were having breakfast the next morning. Mrs. Parfitt was depressed and distrait.

"I wish you'd seen Miss Cummins yesterday, Joan," she said. "I'd like to know whether you felt you were really going to be happy with her. I didn't feel *sure*, but——" she sighed.

"No. I didn't see her at all," said Joan. "William said that that school mistress that's at Ginger's came and tried to join in the game and he told her we didn't want her, but Ginger says she couldn't have because she was at home all day."

But Mrs. Parfitt wasn't listening. She was reading a letter, and her air of dejection was vanishing. The letter was from Miss Cummins and explained that she would not, after all, be able to take Joan into her school next term. Evidently she had made a mistake about numbers and accommodation. She appeared, in fact, not to have known exactly how many pupils she had or how many dormitories. It all boiled down to the fact that she much regretted that she had no room for Joan next term. If there were room later, she would let Mrs. Parfitt know. . . .

"Isn't it lovely!" said Mrs. Parfitt, handing the letter to Joan. "I tried to like her, but I couldn't. It was a beautiful school, but I was miserable whenever I thought of your going there."

"Hurray!" said Joan, reading the letter. "I was trying not to think of it, but whenever I did think of it I simply couldn't bear it."

"And it can't have been anything to do with us," said Mrs. Parfitt, "because she left here with it all settled and she never even saw you."

Joan suddenly remembered the tall, spectacled figure whom William had taken for Ginger's evacuee, though Ginger said that his evacuee had not left the house. William had been wearing her green coat and hat. . . .

"I wonder . . ." she began.

"What, dear?" said Mrs. Parfitt.

But, thinking the matter over, Joan decided that it was one of those cases where you let sleeping dogs lie.

"Oh, nothing," she said.

CHAPTER VII

WILLIAM WORKS FOR PEACE

"I WAS listenin' to someone talkin' at our house the other night," said William, "an' they were talkin' about us all doin' our part for the peace."

"How do you mean, us all doin' our part for the peace?" said Ginger.

"Well, this person said that it wasn't any good expectin' the world to be at peace if we weren't at peace ourselves. He said we'd gotter prepare for the peace by makin' up our own quarrels. He said it would bring peace nearer."

"Sounds batty to me," said Ginger.

"It didn't sound batty the way he said it," said William. "It sounded jolly fine. We've gotter make friends with our enemies an' reconcile people what have quarrelled. He said peace'd come soon if we all did that. Gosh! I'd like peace to come soon. I'm sick of not bein' able to get any bulls' eyes."

"Well, you can't do anythin' about it," objected Ginger.

"Yes, I can. He said everybody could. He said we'd all gotter make friends with enemies an' then peace'd come soon."

"What're you goin' to do, then?" said Ginger. "Are you goin' to make friends with Hubert Lane?"

William considered this suggestion in silence for some moments, then said simply:

"No, I'd rather keep Hubert Lane for an enemy."

"Then you can't do anythin'," said Ginger triumphantly.

"Yes, I can," persisted William. "I can reconcile someone else what's enemies. That counts as much as making friends with an enemy yourself. Anyway, I want Hubert Lane for an enemy, so I'm goin' to do someone else instead."

"Who're you goin' to do?" demanded Ginger.

"Dunno yet," said William. "I've gotter think. Who is there who's quarrelled?"

"There's Miss Milton an' Mrs. Bott," said Ginger.

"Gosh, yes!" said William with interest. "I forgot them. Yes, they'd do fine."

"You'll have a job reconcilin' them," said Ginger doubtfully. "They've been at it a good long time."

Miss Milton and Mrs. Bott had not been on speaking terms for several months. The breach had arisen from trivial causes, as such breaches usually do. There had been the little matter of Mrs. Bott's summarily dismissing a proposal of Miss Milton's at a meeting of the Committee of the Church Rooms Canteen. There had been another little matter of Mrs. Bott's housemaid's repeating to Miss Milton's charwoman various derogatory remarks that she had heard Mrs. Bott make about Miss Milton—remarks that the charwoman had thought fit to report, suitably embellished, to Miss Milton. There had been various other little matters, all slight in themselves, but causing the coldness between the two ladies to increase to open hostility. Neither now acknowledged the existence of the other.

They sat on the same committees, they passed each other regularly in the village street and magnificently ignored each other. Each had given a small tea-party purposely in order not to invite the other. . . .

"I bet I manage it all right," said William. "I've never tried reconcilin' anyone, but I bet it's easy enough once you start."

"I dunno how you're goin' to start," said Ginger. "'Tisn't as if they liked you. . . ."

Even William had to admit that he was not popular with either of the two ladies.

"They're mean ole things, both of 'em," he said. "Jus' as if I meant to scare Miss Milton's rotten ole cat or break those cucumber frames in ole Mrs. Bott's garden. Why, I make that noise at ole Miss Milton's cat to cheer it up. 'Tisn't my fault if it doesn't want to be cheered up. An' I was practisin' walking on a tree branch when I fell into those rotten ole frames. Gosh! You'd've thought she'd be sorry for me cuttin' myself 'stead of carryin' on like what she did. Anyway," firmly, "I'm goin' to reconcile 'em whether they want it or not. I'm goin' to do my bit for the peace same as what this man said. I'm sick of not bein' able to get any bulls' eyes."

"Yes, I know," said Ginger, "I feel the same as what you do about bulls' eyes, but I don't see how reconcilin' 'em's goin' to start bulls' eyes again, an' I don't see how you're goin' to reconcile 'em. I think you'd better stick to things you can do, same as fightin' an' such-like, an' not try this peace stuff."

"Huh!" said William. "You'll think a bit different when I've done it an' peace comes an' you can get bulls' eyes again. You wait! I'm jolly good at ideas."

And, sure enough, William got his idea. That afternoon his mother took him to the pictures to see "Target for To-night" and by a strange coincidence the other picture was the story of the quarrel of two women and their final reconciliation. One was the mother of a winsome, curly-headed child, the other saved the child from an express train, and the two embraced tearfully over the winsome curly head. . . .

William was very silent on the way home. Everything fitted in amazingly. Violet Elizabeth Bott was about the same size as the child in the picture. She was curly-headed and, in the opinion of most people, though not of William, winsome. It only remained for Miss Milton to rescue Violet Elizabeth Bott from an express train. The details might present minor difficulties, but William was not to be balked by minor difficulties.

Violet Elizabeth Bott, when approached, was inclined to be recalcitrant.

"But I don't want to be rethcued from a train," she objected, her habitual lisp accentuated by resentment at the suggestion. "I don't want to be."

"Goodness!" said William sternly. "Fancy not wantin' to be rescued from a train. Fancy wantin' to be run over!"

"I don't want to be run over," said Violet Elizabeth.

"Well, you've gotter be rescued, then," said William. Violet Elizabeth looked slightly bewildered.

"I don't thee why," she said at last simply.

"Now, listen," said William patiently. "You want the war to end so's you can get," he remembered her weakness, "acid drops again, don't you?"

"I can get athid dropth *thometimes* now," said Violet Elizabeth.

"Yes, but you can't get 'em every Saturday same as you used to, can you?" said William.

"No," admitted Violet Elizabeth.

"Well, then, you want the war to end so that you can. Well, this man said that we'd never get peace between nations till we'd got peace between ourselves. He kept on sayin' it. So we've gotter make peace between Miss Milton and your mother."

"My mother dothen't want peath with Mith Milton," said Violet Elizabeth. "Thee thays thee's a nathty dithagreeable old woman."

"Well, she won't feel like that when Miss Milton's rescued you from a train."

"But I don't want to be rethcued from a train," persisted Violet Elizabeth, bringing the conversation round to its starting point.

"Now, listen," said William. "All you've gotter do is to lie down between the lines. Then if the train *does* go over you it won't hurt you. I've often read tales of people lyin' down between the lines an' the trains don't hurt them. They go straight over 'em. Anyway, I'll fetch Miss Milton an' she'll pull you out an' take you to your mother an' then they'll kiss each other."

"An' thall I have loth an' *loth* of athid dropth to-morrow morning?"

"Well, I don't know about that," said William doubtfully. "I expect you'd have to wait a bit."

"Well, I'm not goin' to, anyway," said Violet Elizabeth with unexpected firmness. "I don't like trainth. It maketh me thick to be in them. I ecthpect it'd make me thicker lying between the lineth. An' I'd get all dirty an' methy. I'm not *goin'* to."

"All right," said William, realising that compromise

"ALL YOU'VE GOTTER DO IS TO LIE DOWN BETWEEN THE
LINES," SAID WILLIAM.

was called for at this point. "All right. You needn't
lie between the lines. Listen. You jus' stay near the
lines. On the bank, if you like. An' I'll take your hat
to Miss Milton an' say I found it on the lines. An'
then she'll come runnin' down an' find you lyin' near
the lines an' she'll think you've been knocked down
by the train. You can be moanin' an' groanin' an'
she'll take you home an' your mother'll kiss her."

"I than't have to kith her, thall I?" asked Violet
Elizabeth anxiously. "I don't like her fathe."

"No, you needn't kiss her," William reassured her.
"I bet I wouldn't want to kiss her either. Now, come
on. All you've gotter do is to let me have your hat an'
lie down on the edge of the railway bank moanin' an'
groanin' an' carryin' on an' sayin' "Where am I?"
same as people do when they've had an accident.
Miss Milton's house is just near the railway line, you
know, so you won't have to wait long."

Despite herself, Violet Elizabeth was becoming interested in the idea. Games with William were never
devoid of excitement, and time happened to be hanging
heavy on her hands. She might as well do that as
anything. . . .

      *   *   *   *   *

Miss Milton herself opened the door to William and
stood, stern and unsmiling, gazing down at him.
William was no favourite with Miss Milton.

"Well?" she said grimly.

William held up Violet Elizabeth's brown cloth hat,
in which he had thoughtfully made a dent intended
to represent the wheel of a train.

"I found this on the railway line," he said. "It's
Violet Elizabeth's. An' Violet Elizabeth's lyin' jus'

near where I found it moanin' an' groanin' as if she'd been run over by a train."

For a moment Miss Milton looked startled. Then her eye caught Violet Elizabeth's rosy face peeping over the hedge at the bottom of the garden. For Violet Elizabeth was a self-centred child and wished to witness the gratifying spectacle of Miss Milton's distress on hearing of her accident. She thought that she could easily slip down to the railway line again in time to receive Miss Milton with the moans and groans in which William had painstakingly instructed her. . . .

"You *naughty* boy!" said Miss Milton severely. "How *dare* you play such tricks on me?" and slammed the door.

William turned round in amazement to see Violet Elizabeth's face peeping over the hedge.

"You've gone and spoilt it all," he compained when he rejoined her. "What on earth did you want to do that for?"

"I only wanted to thee what thee looked like when thee thought I'd been run over," apologised Violet Elizabeth humbly. "I'm thorry, William."

"Well, we'll have to think up somethin' else now," said William. "What about you bein' drowned?"

Violet Elizabeth paled.

"I don't want to be drowned, William," she objected, then, her indignation increasing and her perception of the issues at stake becoming slightly confused, added with spirit: "Why thould I be drowned juth soth you can have athid dropth on Thaturdayth? You're very thelfith, William."

"It's *you* I'm tryin' to get acid drops for," said William impatiently, "an' you needn't even get wet.

L

I'll jus' put your hat in water an' make it all drippin'
an' take it to her an' say I found it floatin' on the pond
an' she'll go flyin' to your mother an'—an' kiss her.   It
won't matter them findin' out you've not been drowned
afterwards, 'cause they'll have made friends by then
an' everythin'll be all right."

Rather reluctantly Violet Elizabeth agreed.   William
dipped her hat in the rain tub and took it dripping to
Miss Milton's front door.

"Please I found this——" began William, but with
a "Go away at *once* and don't dare to come here again
or I'll tell your father," Miss Milton once more slammed
the door in his face.   Miss Milton was not in a mood to
be trifled with.   She was feeling harassed and worried.
It was one of those days when, as she put it, "everything comes at once."   Her cousin Julia had arranged
some weeks ago to run over and spend the afternoon
with her.   Another more distant cousin, whose husband had been posted to Marleigh aerodrome from
the North of England and who was moving into a
small house just outside the village, had rung up to ask
if her two children might come to tea this afternoon
with Miss Milton in order to get them out of the way
while she "settled in."   And—to crown all—the War
Working Party which generally took place at the
Vicarage on Thursday had been changed to this afternoon.   And Miss Milton did not want to miss the War
Working Party, because Mrs. Bott would be there, and
Miss Milton did not want Mrs. Bott to think that she
was frightened of her.   She wanted to go to the working
party and ignore Mrs. Bott as magnificently as Mrs.
Bott ignored her.   And, with her cousin and the two
children coming to tea, how could she?

Quite suddenly yesterday evening the solution of the problem had occurred to her. She would ask Julia to entertain the children, so that she could go to the working party. Julia was one of those amiable kind-hearted people who are willing to do anything for anyone, and, moreover, had the reputation of being fond of children, which Miss Milton most emphatically was not. That solved the problem, but still Miss Milton was worried. She had never seen Douglas and Susan, the two children, before and she didn't know what they were like. They were probably unruly and destructive, like all other children, and Julia probably wouldn't have any control over them. People who were fond of children never had. . . . She trembled to think of a couple of unruly destructive children let loose in her spotless little house. Better that, however, than that Mrs. Bott should think she was afraid of her. . . .

And, as if all these complications weren't enough, that unspeakable Brown boy had to choose to-day to play his tricks on her. . . .

"It wasn't any good," said William, rejoining Violet Elizabeth in the road. "She didn't seem to care whether you were drowned or not."

"An' a nithe meth you've made of my hat!" said Violet Elizabeth, looking at the dripping object severely. "It wath an ecthpenthive hat."

"Well, I did my best," said William. "I'm only tryin' to stop the war same as everyone else. Goodness! Fancy you makin' a fuss about a hat, when you think of all the money Churchill's spendin' on it! You don't deserve to get the war stopped an' have acid drops."

"Yeth, I do," pleaded Violet Elizabeth. "I only thaid you'd made a meth of it. You *have* made a meth of it."

"Well, never mind the hat," said William. "We've gotter think what to do next."

Anyone less determined than William would have

"WELL I DID MY BEST," SAID WILLIAM. "I'M ONLY TRYIN' TO STOP THE WAR SAME AS EVERYONE ELSE."

abandoned that particular plan of reconciliation, but William did not abandon his plans lightly.

"I bet she got so mad 'cause she saw me," he said. "She doesn't like me. . . . If she jus' saw you dyin' or faintin' or somethin' without me there I bet she'd run out to help."

"I don't want to die," objected Violet Elizabeth plaintively. "I keep tellin' you I don't. You won't lithen."

"An' I keep tellin' you you needn't do it really," said William. "It's jus' pretendin'. Look! You go an' lie down at the bottom of her garden without movin', an' when she comes out to you jus' go on lyin' there without movin' or speakin'——"

"Can't I thay 'where am I'? pleaded Violet Elizabeth.

"No, you'll only mess it up if you start speakin'. Jus' go on lyin' there with your eyes shut. Then she'll ring up your mother an' your mother'll come an'—an' they'll make it up an' kiss each other.

"An' give me athid dropth," added Violet Elizabeth happily.

"Yes," agreed William, "as soon as this peace gets goin'. I'll come an' help you lie down. You've not gotter lie straight out. You've gotter lie all crumpled up jus' as if you'd gone faint an' fell all of a heap. We'll do it now. It's all right. She's round at the other side of the house in the kitchen."

There was a certain amount of difficulty in deciding the exact posture which Violet Elizabeth should adopt. Now that the central position in the tableau was to be hers, she assumed the air of a temperamental prima donna and peevishly rejected all William's suggestions.

"I can't lie all thquathed up like that," she said.

"I thall get pinth an' needleth. I'm goin' to lie thame ath I lie in bed when I'm athleep. If I've got to thay here hourth an' hourth till thee thees me out of the window I'm not goin' to be all thquathed up an' uncomfortable."

It was while the altercation was going on—William standing up and Violet Elizabeth sitting on the grass, both gesticulating fiercely to prove their points—that Miss Milton went into her sitting-room and saw them through the window. She flung the window open, her face flushed with anger.

"Go out of my garden at *once*, you naughty children!" she said. "I shall most certainly complain to your parents."

William realised the explanation would be worse than useless.

"Oh, come on!" he said to Violet Elizabeth. "You've messed *that* up now."

"I don't care," said Violet Elizabeth. "I'm not goin' to be all thquathed up—not for anyone. Anyway ith lunth time an' I'm hungry. I'm goin' home."

"All right," said William. "Go home! I don't want you. You're a soppy conceited ole girl an' you've jolly well messed the whole thing up an' I'm sick of you."

"An' you're a thtupid dithagreeable boy an' I'm thick of you," retorted Violet Elizabeth with spirit.

Despite the interchange of personalities, however, neither really wanted to leave the adventure in this half-finished condition.

"I'll try 'n' think somethin' else out while I'm havin' lunch," said William. "You meet me at your gate after lunch an' I bet I'll have thought somethin' else out."

"All right," said Violet Elizabeth, accepting the

tacit overture, "an' I'll try'n' think thomething elth out too."

Oddly enough, it was Violet Elizabeth who had the idea.

"I remembered it juth ath I was eating rith pudding an' pruneth," she said. "It came to me thuddenly. I gueth you'll thay ith a good idea. I gueth ith better than yourth. . . ."

"Yes, but what *is* it?" said William impatiently.

"It wath a thtory I oneth read," explained Violet Elizabeth. "It wath a thoppy thtory, but I gueth ith a good idea. There wath a little girl in the thtory an' thee lotht her memory an' thee went to a houth an' thaid to the woman, 'Pleath, are you my mummy?' An' thith woman wath thad an' lonely an' the little girl thtayed an' comforted her till her real mummy found her an' her mummy an' thith woman were friendth alwayth afterwardth. It wath a thoppy thtory but——"

William saw the point. It was a soppy story but . . . Violet Elizabeth arriving at Miss Milton's cottage and saying: "Pleath, are you my mummy?" Miss Milton and Mrs. Bott friends always afterwards. . . . Peace. . . . Acid drops. . . . Bulls' eyes. . . . The other plans had gone wrong, he was convinced, because he had appeared with Violet Elizabeth. In this he need not appear at all. . . .

"It's not bad," he said, carefully tempering his enthusiasm lest Violet Elizabeth should get above herself, as she was inclined to. "No, it's not bad. We might manage it all right. . . . It's not *bad*. . . ."

"Ith good," said Violet Elizabeth with calm conviction. "Ith very good. An' ith eathy."

"It's not as easy as you think," said William. "You can't jus' walk in an' say that. You've gotter *act* like someone what's lost their mem'ry. Can you *act* like someone what's lost their mem'ry?"

"No," admitted Violet Elizabeth. "Thith thtory didn't thay anythin' about that."

"Well, you'll have to have a bit of practice first, then," said William, who by this time had completely adopted the idea as his own. "People what've lost their mem'ries carry on in a special sort of way. Like this. . . ."

He assumed an imbecile expression, allowed his head to drop forward, his mouth to drop open and lurched unsteadily across the road. "You'll need a bit of practice," he repeated. "Let's practise down this road a bit first. You watch me and do everything I do."

He reassumed his imbecile expression, dropped his head forward, his mouth open, and began to lurch down the road. Violet Elizabeth imitated him as best she could with earnest concentration. So intent were they on the proceeding that they did not see two children coming from the opposite direction—a boy of about William's size and a girl about Violet Elizabeth's—till they had nearly collided with them. The four of them stood and stared at each other.

"What's your name?" said the boy.

William, throwing an admonitory glance at Violet Elizabeth as if to call her attention to the object lesson, gaped at the boy with open mouth and said:

"Dunno."

"Gosh!" said the boy, taken aback. He turned to Violet Elizabeth.

"What's yours?" he said.

"WHAT'S YOUR NAME?" SAID THE BOY.

"Dunno," said Violet Elizabeth, giving a faithful imitation of William's performance.

"Crumbs!" said the boy.

"How old are you?" he said to William.

"Dunno," said William.

"Well, how old are *you*?" he said to Violet Elizabeth.

"Dunno," said Violet Elizabeth, improving on William's performance by letting her tongue loll out of her mouth too.

"Corks!" said the boy with growing amazement. "Don't you know your name or how old you are?"

"I've lost my memory," said William.

"I've lotht mine, too," said Violet Elizabeth.

The boy had worn a dejected expression when they first met him, but now he brightened suddenly.

"I say, Susan," he said, drawing the girl aside. "I've got an idea."

They whispered together, while William and Violet Elizabeth, warming to their task, gaped and lolled and lurched about the road. At last the boy approached them.

"Look here!" he said kindly. "It's lucky for you you met us because we know who you are. You're a brother and sister and you're called Douglas and Susan Keith, and you're going to tea with a lady called Miss Milton. We know where she lives, too, so we'll take you to her. . . . You're jolly lucky to have met us. You'll be all right now."

William was too much taken aback to resist. Moreover, having sustained the character of a boy who had lost his memory so effectively, he was reluctant to abandon it. After all, they were going to Miss Milton's, and it was there that the next step in the proceedings was due to take place, anyway. He'd manage somehow to slip away when they arrived at Miss Milton's, so that Violet Elizabeth could go in alone, repeat her little piece and lead on to the great reconciliation scene. The other two wore a jubilant air as they walked on either side like a bodyguard. The appearance of these two children, of about the same age as themselves, who had so conveniently lost their memories, was a god-send. The prospect of having to waste the glorious hours of the first day in a new home going to tea with an elderly and unknown relative, when they might be roaming the countryside and exploring the woods that stretched so temptingly on all sides, had weighed heavily on their spirits. Now they were saved. This odd couple without memories would take their place, and Miss Milton, who had never seen them before, would be satisfied. Later complications they were content to leave to fate. . . . At least they would have had this wonderful first day for exploring. No other day is quite like the first. . . .

They coached their substitutes assiduously as they shepherded them along the road.

"Your father's a Flight Lieutenant at Marleigh Aerodrome."

"You've only just moved there. You've gone to a furnished house near the aerodrome and your mother's busy settling in to-day."

"You've got an Aunt Lucy and an Uncle Herbert and they're both quite well if this Miss Milton asks after 'em."

"You're all quite well if Miss Milton asks after them."

"Uncle Herbert had an operation last year, but he's quite all right again."

"An' you had measles in the spring, but you're quite all right again."

"An' don't forget your names. You're Douglas an' Susan Keith."

"Jolly good thing for you you met someone that knows you!"

"An' your mother told you to give Miss Milton her love. Don't forget that."

They had reached Miss Milton's cottage now.

"This must be it," said the boy. "Third on the right past the church. Yes, this must be it. Well, go straight up an' knock at the door an' say you're Douglas an' Susan, an' I hope you have a good time."

With that the couple turned and ran back as fast as they could down the road, giving kangaroo-like leaps of exultation as they went.

William and Violet Elizabeth stood at the gate of the cottage, bewildered by this unexpected turn of events. William was the first to recover.

"Never mind them," he said. "They're batty. You go in same as you were going to an' carry on same as we've been practisin' an' say 'Please, are you my——'"

But it was too late. Already a strange lady—not Miss Milton but with an elusive likeness to her—was bearing down on them from the front door.

"*There* you are!" she said with an all-embracing smile of welcome. "It's Douglas and Susan, isn't it? Come along in. I'm Miss Milton's cousin, so I'm a sort of relation, too. You must call me Aunt Julia. Miss Milton's gone to her working party and left me to entertain you. Come along."

Events were moving too quickly for William. Before he could recover his forces, he found himself swept up to the cottage door and into the cottage. And there he stood and stared in amazement. For, spread on the table was a tea such as he had not seen for months. Miss Julia Milton, informed the day before that she was to entertain the children to tea and aware that her cousin's preparations would be on a niggardly scale, had determined to supply deficiencies and give the "poor little souls" a real treat. She had used all her precious store of pre-war icing sugar and made a large and luscious-looking chocolate cake. She had bought chocolate biscuits and a bottle of orange squash. She had made jellies.

"I thought I'd contribute my share," she explained apologetically to Miss Milton when she arrived, her little car loaded up with dainties.

Miss Milton had looked at her cargo sourly.

"Well, of course," she had said distantly, "if you *want* to waste time and money on a couple of ungrateful badly-behaved children——"

"How do you know they're ungrateful and badly behaved?" said Miss Julia. "You've never met them."

"All children are ungrateful and badly behaved," said Miss Milton simply.

"I'm sure Douglas and Susan aren't," said Miss Julia confidently.

She had spent a happy half-hour since Miss Milton's departure to her working party, arranging the table and setting out cake, biscuits and jellies.

"*Oh!*" said Violet Elizabeth as her eyes fell on it, and

"*Corks!*" said William.

By tacit consent they decided to put off explanations till after tea.

They remembered that tea afterwards as one of the few bright spots of the war. It wasn't only the cakes and biscuits and jellies, delicious as they were. It was Miss Julia Milton, who turned out to be unlike her cousin in every way. In order to put them at their ease she told them stories of her own childhood and that of her brothers and sisters, describing their pranks and adventures so vividly and humorously that William and Violet Elizabeth chuckled with delight. Tea-time passed without a hitch. No awkward questions were

"*OH!*" SAID VIOLET ELIZABETH AS HER EYES FELL ON THE TABLE.

asked, no awkward references made. . . . Occasionally William and Violet Elizabeth were slow to respond to the names of Douglas and Susan, but no other demands were made on them beyond eating the cakes and biscuits and jellies.

"And you'll help me clear away and wash up, won't you?" said Miss Julia when her guests could eat no more, "then everything will be nice and clean and straight when Miss Milton comes home."

They helped her clear away and wash up, and Miss Julia told them more stories about her childhood. She had evidently been an adventurous child, and even William mentally pigeon-holed a few ideas from her exploits for future use. Once, when Miss Julia had gone outside to shake the cloth and they were alone in the sitting-room, Violet Elizabeth, suddenly remembering the point from which the strange situation had developed, said: "Thall I athk her if thee's my mummy now, William?"

"Gosh, no!" said William. "That'd spoil everythin'. Besides, this isn't the right one. We'll have to wait till the right one gets back. . . . I bet it won't come off now, anyway, but I don't care. It was the best tea I've had since the war."

"What shall we play at first?" said Miss Julia, coming back into the room and putting the table-cloth away in a drawer in the sideboard. "You choose, Susan."

"Hide an' theek," said Violet Elizabeth promptly.

But suddenly Miss Julia's pleasant, smiling face clouded over.

"Oh dear, I forgot!" she said. "My cousin particularly asked me to post a letter for her. It's about an order for wool for the War Working Party. I know she wants it to go to-day. I tell you what. I'll leave you here to find really good hiding-places while I go to the post office and when I come back I'll start looking for you at once. That'll be all right, won't it? Well, good-bye for the present."

"Good-bye," said William and Violet Elizabeth.

"You hide upstairs," said William to Violet Elizabeth when she had gone, "an' I'll hide downstairs. I bet she finds you first. Girls can't ever find decent hiding-places."

"Oh, can't they?" said Violet Elizabeth. "Juth you wait an' thee."

A few minutes later Miss Milton, Mrs. Bott, Mrs. Brown and Mrs. Monks arrived at the cottage. The War Working Party was over, and they had called at Miss Milton's for more wool on their way home. Miss Milton, as secretary of the War Working Party, had charge of the wool and was, Mrs. Bott considered, unduly officious over it. But Mrs. Bott, though she had, while still magnificently ignoring Miss Milton, managed to make several offensive allusions to her in her hearing and would normally have been feeling very pleased with herself about it, was distrait and worried. For, shortly before the meeting broke up, the maid in whose charge Violet Elizabeth had been left had telephoned to say that she had seen nothing of her since lunch and that she had not been home for tea. Mrs. Bott, still studiously ignoring Miss Milton, was confiding her anxieties to Mrs. Monks and Mrs. Brown alternately, and dropping her aitches more wildly even than usual in her anxiety.

"I can't think what's 'appened to the child," she

said. "I've told her most particular not to go on the main roads an' she never does. I will say that for 'er. She's as scared of traffic as what I am myself. I can't understand 'er not comin' 'ome to tea even if she'd been off playin' with someone. She knew Cook 'ad made a sponge cake an' she's crazy on sponge cakes."

"I'm sure she's all right, Mrs. Bott," Mrs. Monks reassured her.

"I wish I was," said Mrs. Bott. "One 'ears of such things! Children kidnapped an' all."

"No one would kidnap her, Mrs. Bott," said Mrs. Brown.

"Oh, wouldn't they?" said Mrs. Bott still more darkly.

"You've no enemies or anything of that sort."

Mrs. Bott couldn't resist this opening and shot a malignant glance at Miss Milton.

"Oh, 'aven't I?" she said. "''Aven't I, indeed? A certain person knows whether I 'ave or not."

"Come, come Mrs. Bott," said Mrs. Monks briskly. "This won't do. Now let's get the wool business settled up and then I'll go back to the Hall with you and we'll have a good hunt for Violet Elizabeth. I expect she's somewhere in the house or garden all the time, but if we can't find her I'll get my bicycle and go down to the village and ask if anyone's seen her there. . . . The first thing to do is to get the wool distributed. I want some more oiled sea-boot stocking wool, Miss Milton. Is there any left?"

"Oh, some came the other day," said Miss Milton, "and there wasn't room in the cupboard, so I put it up in the boxroom. I'll get it."

"No, I'll get it," said Mrs. Monks. "I know where

M

the boxroom is. You go on giving out the other wool. We want to get through the business quickly, then I can help poor Mrs. Bott find her missing girlie. I won't be a moment."

Complacently aware that she was handling a difficult situation with tact and discretion, Mrs. Monks made her way up to the little boxroom. There were the balls of oiled wool on an old-fashioned leather trunk. Mrs. Monks took them, and was on the point of going out of the room when she was arrested by a sound. It was an odd, rhythmic sound rather like a snore. Mrs. Monks listened again. It seemed to come from the ceiling above her head. It might be the cistern, of course. It probably was the cistern. But it was unlike any other cistern that Mrs. Monks had ever heard. It was much more like a snore—a small gentle snore. Mrs. Monks looked up at the ceiling, in which there was a trap-door leading into the loft. The trap-door was closed, but by it, resting on a pile of old trunks, was a ladder. Mrs. Monks hesitated a moment, then on an impulse took up the ladder and fitted the hooks at the end into the sockets that were fixed just beneath the trap-door. She mounted cautiously, opened the trap-door, and glanced round the little loft. At first she couldn't believe her eyes—for there, curled up on the dusty cobwebby floor and sound asleep, was Violet Elizabeth Bott. Violet Elizabeth, stung by William's parting taunt, had determined to find a hiding-place that should baffle even William himself. She had found the ladder fixed to its hooks, had gone up to the loft, dropped the ladder on to a pile of trunks, closed the trap-door and sat down to await events. But the excitement of the afternoon and the large tea of which she had just partaken had made her drowsy and before she knew what was happening she had dropped sound asleep, dreaming of William and Miss Julia and iced chocolate cake and emitting the gentle little snore that was the result of a slight tendency to adenoids.

Mrs. Monks stood, her head just above the aperture of the trap-door, and stared. . . . She still could hardly believe her eyes, but there it was. She *had* to believe them. How or why Miss Milton had kidnapped the child and imprisoned her in her loft she didn't know, but there was no other possible explanation. The quarrel between Mrs. Bott and Miss Milton had been the talk of the village for months past, and certainly Miss Milton had had a good deal to put up with from Mrs. Bott, who could be devastatingly and almost incredibly rude, but it seemed unbelievable that she should have stooped to a revenge like this. Still, Mrs. Monks had read books on psychology and knew that elderly spinsters did queer things. Miss Milton must have brooded on her quarrel with Mrs. Bott till it had turned her brain. . . .

"Violet Elizabeth!" she said in an urgent whisper.

The urgent whisper penetrated Violet Elizabeth's dreams, and William turned into a monster bottle of acid drops.

"Violet Elizabeth," said Mrs. Monks again.

Violet Elizabeth sat up and blinked. Her usually tidy curls were rumpled and she was covered with dust and cobwebs.

"You poor child!" said Mrs. Monks, compassionately. "What a dreadful experience for you! There's nothing to be afraid of any more, dear. I'm here and I'm going to take you back to Mummy. . . . Come along."

Violet Elizabeth, still half asleep, allowed herself

to be helped down the ladder and drawn gently along the landing and down the stairs. Mrs. Monks wondered whether to tidy her up a bit, then decided that it

"I HAVE JUST RESCUED HER. OH, MISS MILTON,"
SAID MRS. MONKS, "HOW *COULD* YOU!"

"I DON'T KNOW WHAT YOU'RE TALKING ABOUT,"
GASPED MISS MILTON.

would be best to let the witnesses downstairs see her fresh
from the rigours of her kidnapping and imprisonment.

She entered the room and stood for a moment in
the doorway so that they could not see Violet Elizabeth,
who was just behind her.

"Mrs. Bott," she said, "I have found Violet Elizabeth."

"Found Violet Elizabeth?" repeated Mrs. Bott in amazement.

"Yes. I have found her imprisoned in Miss Milton's loft," said Mrs. Monks, standing aside to reveal the crumpled cobwebby figure of Violet Elizabeth. "I have just rescued her. Oh, Miss Milton," turning to her hostess, "how *could* you!"

"I don't know what you're talking about," gasped Miss Milton. "You must be mad. I've never set eyes on her till this moment since she was playing round here this morning."

"It's useless to deny it," said Mrs. Monks firmly but sorrowfully. "We are all witnesses and—look at the state the poor child's in!"

Mrs. Bott clasped the small cobwebby figure to her ample bosom.

"My poor child!" she moaned. "'Ow you must 'ave suffered!" Then, turning to Miss Milton, her whole plump body quivering with rage: "As for you—you in'uman monster, you'll pay for this. You see if you don't. Me an' Botty'll sue you for kidnappin' an'—an' assault an'—an' cruelty to children an' we won't rest till we've got you jailed—not if we 'ave to spend our last penny on it."

"But—but, Mrs. Bott——" began Miss Milton. She had sat down weakly on a chair and was on the verge of tears. "I assure you I know nothing of this. Nothing whatever. . . ."

Mrs. Bott had again enveloped Violet Elizabeth in the ample maternal bosom.

"Did she hurt you, my precious?"

"No, thee din't hurt me," said Violet Elizabeth, still half asleep, then, dimly remembering how the whole thing had started: "Can I have an athid drop now?"

"As many as you like, my pet," said Mrs. Bott and added: "At least, if we can get the things."

At this moment Miss Julia Milton entered breathlessly.

"I'm sorry I've been so long," she said, smiling round at the company. "What *will* the children think of me! But I met the Vicar and he was telling me all about the evacuees' camp and——"

She stopped, vaguely aware that something was wrong.

"Where are Douglas and Susan?" said Miss Milton anxiously, hoping that she hadn't imprisoned them in the loft, too.

Miss Julia looked at Violet Elizabeth.

"Well, here's Susan and"—as William, drawn from his hiding-place by the sound of raised voices, appeared suddenly in the doorway—"and here's Douglas."

"William!" moaned Mrs. Brown.

She had just been congratulating herself that at least William could have no hand in this, but here he was, as usual, at the heart of the trouble.

The others stared in stupefied silence, and at that moment the door opened and in came a tall woman in a tweed suit.

"Sorry to barge in," she said, "but I thought a little walk would do me good, and I've called for Susan and Douglas."

"Well, there they are," said Miss Julia, pointing to

Violet Elizabeth and William. "I'm sorry you've come so early. We were looking forward to a little game of hide and seek."

"We're 'avin' it all right," said Mrs. Bott darkly. "What I want to know is, what's been goin' on in this 'ouse?"

"But where *are* Susan and Douglas?" said their mother to Miss Milton.

"I don't know," said Miss Milton. "I don't know anything. I think I'm going mad."

One would have thought that the situation could not become more complicated than it was at that point. But it could and it did. For Violet Elizabeth, emerging slowly from the mists of sleep and remembering more clearly what had led up to the situation, felt that her moment had come. She stepped up to Miss Milton and said:

"Pleath, are you my mummy?"

*   *   *   *   *

"It was an awful mess-up," said William morosely to Ginger. "They were all talkin' at me an' askin' questions at once an' I kep' tryin' to explain. Well, when they'd got it sort of clear, if ole Miss Milton and Mrs. Bott didn't put their arms round each other and kiss each other same as I'd meant them to all along, an' you'd 've thought they'd be a bit grateful to me for reconcilin' them, wouldn't you? But they weren't. Oh no! I'd gone to all that trouble to make 'em friends to get the war over an' they went on at me as if I was ole Hitler himself. I couldn't help ole Violet Elizabeth gettin' stuck in that loft, but everythin's gotter be *my* fault. You should have seen the way my father went on at me! An' Vi'let Elizabeth—jus' 'cause she can't get whole bottles of acid drops the minute her mother an' ole Miss Milton make it up, she's so mad, she won't speak to me. She's a soppy kid, anyway. Oh well, I'm jus' about sick of tryin' to help people an' get the war over. Come on, let's play Red Indians."

CHAPTER VIII

WILLIAM SPENDS A BUSY MORNING

"I DON'T see how I can possibly get it done this year," said Mrs. Brown. "I simply haven't a minute now I've all the cooking on my hands."

"I'll do it for you," volunteered William.

"Oh William, you couldn't!" said Mrs. Brown in undisguised horror.

"Why couldn't I?" challenged William.

"You'd make a mess of it. You make a mess of everything."

"I don't," said William indignantly. "I jolly well don't. There's lots of things I haven't made a mess of. There's—well, I can't think of anythin' at the minute, but I bet there *is* lots of things I haven't made a mess of if I'd got time to think of 'em."

"Well, I'm sure you couldn't do my collecting."

Mrs. Brown was local secretary of a large association for alleviating distress in the London slums and her yearly collecting of the local subscriptions was a tense and nerve-racking affair for the Brown family. She sallied forth every morning armed with her receipt book and a large handbag. She spent each evening adding up and checking her accounts. People were out and she had to go again and again.... Meals were late and Mrs. Brown lost her usual expression of placid good humour—till the subscriptions were finally collected and sent up to headquarters, and the Brown household breathed again.

"I simply haven't the time this year," said Mrs. Brown again. "Now Cook's gone it takes me all my time shopping and seeing to the meals . . . I simply can't face that traipsing round after half-crowns."

"Well, I keep tellin' you I'll do it," said William.

"Of *course* you——" began Mrs. Brown impatiently, then stopped and looked thoughtful. "Well, now I come to think of it, so many people have gone away since the war that there's only about a pound to be collected—all in half-crowns." She looked at him doubtfully. "I wonder if you *could*. . . ."

"'Course I could," said William. "I keep tellin' you I could. Anyway, what could I do wrong?"

"I don't know," said Mrs. Brown simply. "I never do know—till afterwards."

"I'd jus' go to the houses," said William, "an' ask for the half-crowns an' get 'em an' put 'em in my pocket an' bring 'em home. I can't *poss'bly* do it wrong."

"I wish I felt sure," sighed Mrs. Brown. "You'd have to give them receipts, of course, and the annual reports. . . ."

"Well, I could do that all right," said William.

Finally Mrs. Brown yielded, and William set off with eight receipt forms signed by Mrs. Brown, eight annual reports and a large leather purse in which to put his eight half-crowns.

"I expect some of them will be out," said Mrs. Brown, "but you'll do your best, won't you?"

"'Course I will," said William, "an' I bet I come back with 'em, all right."

Fate seemed at first to favour him. He went from

house to house of the eight subscribers. Each was at home, each gave him half a crown and received in return the receipt form, duly made out by Mrs. Brown, and an annual report. He set off homeward with the eight half-crowns firmly fastened in the leather purse and the pocket in which he had carried the reports and receipt forms empty. He walked slowly and thoughtfully. Though the pocket in which he had carried the annual reports was now empty, William had found time between his visits to glance at them and had been appalled by the magnitude of the task to be covered by the eight half-crowns. Drunkards to be reformed, slums to be cleared, the starving to be fed, the homeless housed. . . . Eight half-crowns represented, of course, an immense sum, but even William could see that it was as nothing in face of the task before it. . . .

He sat down on a stile and took out the leather purse. Better count them over once more and make sure they were all there before he took them home. . . . One, two, three, four, five, six, seven, eight . . . yes, they were all there. Pity it wasn't a bit more. . . . He wondered if it would be any good to go round begging on his own account but decided finally that it wouldn't be. Grown-up people never listened to him and children hadn't any money. . . . He was carefully replacing the eight half-crowns in the purse when he looked up suddenly to find a tramp standing by the stile watching him. He was a ragged, dirty tramp with a luxuriant black beard. Except for the twinkle in his eye, he suggested one of those "cases" for which William's half-crowns were ultimately destined. A puppy of indeterminate breed frolicked at his heels.

"Got a lot of money, me lad," he said with a friendly grin. "Couldn't spare a bit for a poor old chap wot's not tasted food for three days, could you?"

William wrestled with the temptation to give him one of the half-crowns and overcame it.

"I'm sorry," he said reluctantly, "but it's not mine.

"GOT A LOT OF MONEY, ME LAD," SAID THE TRAMP
WITH A FRIENDLY GRIN.

It's for poor people, but it's got to go up to London first. Why don't you go up to London an' ask them for some? Or," as another thought struck him, "there's the Vicar. He lives jus' along at the end of this road. He's got a sort of fund for sick an' poor. Dunno if you've gotter be both. I 'spect poor by itself would be all right."

The tramp made a contemptuous gesture and spat into the road.

"Charity!" he said. "I'd sooner starve to death than live on charity. . . . No," he looked down sadly at the puppy that was still frolicking round his heels, "seems to me I'll have to part with 'im, though it'll break me 'eart."

"Sell him, you mean?" said William.

"That's it, young sir. Sell 'im."

William looked at the puppy with interest.

"How much d'you think you'd get for him? He's a mongrel, isn't he?"

The tramp burst into a roar of laughter.

"A mongrel? Him a mongrel?" he repeated. "Why, 'e's one of the most valu'ble dawgs in England. 'E's an Abyssinian Retriever. I've been offered as much as a hundred pounds for him. I don't know that there *is* another in England. They've been in our family since my great grandfather was in Abyssinia an' brought one back, an' since then we've kept 'em in our family. There's dawg fanciers all over England mad to get 'old of one. There's organisations of dawg thieves up to every trick to steal this 'ere one. I daren't let 'im out of my sight for a minute. . . . If you'd told me this time last week that I'd ever sell 'im I'd have laughed at you . . . but—well, I don't think the sort of life I'm leadin's good for a dawg. I'd like the dawg to 'ave a good 'ome for the dawg's sake. You can see for yourself I've come down in the world. It'd surprise you to know the sort of family I started from—butlers an' evenin' dress an' fountings in the garden same as you see in the pictures—but I've 'ad misfortunes, through no fault of me own. I 'aven't got it in me to do a dishonest action an' that's why I've come down in the world. Honest Jim's been me nickname from a child. I've always put others before myself an' that's why I want this 'ere little dawg to 'ave an 'appy 'ome 'owever much I miss 'im. . . . 'Ow much money 'ave you got in that purse of yours?"

"A pound," said William, "but it's not mine. . . ."

"Well, then, don't you spend it, me lad," said the tramp virtuously. "Never spend money that's not your own. That's been my motter through life an' I've never regretted it. Always remember Honest Jim tellin' you that. . . . But, mind you, there's nothin' against you buyin' somethin' with that there pound that you know you can sell again for more. Then you'll 'ave your pound back *an'* a good bit besides. . . ."

William considered. He was anxious to do something to help his mother's society. The one pound he carried in his purse still seemed pitifully inadequate to provide comfort for the aged, homes for the homeless, food for the starving. . . .

"How much are you selling the dog for?" said William.

The tramp looked at him speculatively.

"Well, it depends 'oo it's to," he said. "Most people I'd ask a 'undred pounds for 'im, but I've took a liking to you. I've never met a boy I've took such a liking to as I've took to you. You're honest, same as what I am myself. Most people would think I'm a fool, but I've got a soft 'eart an' I'm not ashamed of it an' when I makes a friend I likes to treat 'im as such. Now don't laugh at me—but I'll let you 'ave that there little dawg for as little as a pound."

William considered this, his freckled face set and frowning. He was deeply touched by the tramp's generosity, but he was still not completely lost to sanity.

"I might not be able to sell it," he said. "People haven't got much money jus' now 'cause of the war, an' there's not many dog places round here. There's only Emmett's in Hadley an'——"

"Emmett's in 'Adley!" repeated the tramp, with a short surprised laugh. "Well, if that don't beat all! I was down in 'Adley this mornin' an' I was walkin' past the shop when out come Emmett 'isself. 'E sez, 'Ow much d'you want for that Abyssinian Retriever?' 'e sez, an' I sez 'A 'undred pound,' I sez, an' he sez, 'Well, it's less than it's worth,' 'e sez. 'I've bin tryin' to get an Abyssinian Retriever for years. But what with the war an' all, fifty pound down's all I could give you, an' I'd give you that this very minute if you'd let me 'ave the dawg,' 'e sez. 'Well, I'm not sellin' at the minute,' I sez. 'I'll let you know when I am,' I sez. 'An' I'll 'ave fifty pound ready an' waitin',' 'e sez."

William opened his mouth to speak when the tramp hastily interrupted him.

"I 'spect you're wonderin' why I din't go back to 'im when I made up me mind to sell the dawg. Well, I din't want to tell you about that, 'cause I can see you've got a soft 'eart, but I s'pose I'd better. Well,

I've 'eard since then that me pore ole mother's very ill an' askin' for me so I've not time to go down to 'Adley. I'm hurryin' 'ome to me pore ole mother. An' I mustn't stay 'ere chatterin' any longer, young sir, spite of the fancy I've took to you. Juty calls, an' Honest Jim's never been deaf to the call of juty. Now make up your mind quick. Either you want to turn one pound into fifty or you don't. 'And it over an' take the dawg or I mus' find someone else an' get on to me pore ole mother. I'd like you to 'ave it. I'll regret it almost as much as you if you don't, 'cause of this fancy I've took to you. An' you'll regret it the rest of your life. Well, I can't stop no longer so——"

"All right," said William breathlessly. "I'll take it. You—you're *sure* I can get fifty pounds for it at Emmett's?"

The tramp looked at him reproachfully.

"I'm surprised at you askin' that, young sir. Honest Jim's never spoke a word of untruth in 'is life. All you've gotter do is to go into Emmett's with the little dawg an' say "Ere's Honest Jim's Abyssinian Retriever,' an' come out with fifty pounds in your 'and, but if you don't b'lieve me——"

"Yes, I do believe you," said William hastily. "It's all right. . . ." He took out the leather purse, poured the eight half-crowns into his grimy palm and carefully counted them into the tramp's still grimier one.

"Well, that's the best bargain you'll ever get in your life," said Honest Jim. He picked up the puppy, put it into William's arms, pocketed the eight half-crowns and with a "Go'-bye, young sir. You're in luck's way to-day," set off jauntily and somewhat hurriedly down the road.

N

"PLEASE, I'VE BROUGHT HONEST JIM'S ABYSSINIAN
RETRIEVER," SAID WILLIAM.

William looked at his purchase. It was an attractive
puppy—brown and plump and friendly. An Abyssinian Retriever . . . worth a hundred pounds. He put
it down on the ground. It seemed to accept him as its
new master with exuberant delight, jumping up at
him and uttering sharp, shrill excited barks. Had
William's heart not been given to his own dog Jumble
(engaged at the moment on an illicit marauding ex-
pedition in the neighbouring woods) he would have
found it hard to part from this new friend. But he
watched the friskings and leapings with an absent

expression, his brow furrowed by thought. An Abyssinian Retriever . . . worth a hundred pounds. There was a small cold doubt in his mind that he dared not face. . . .

"Well, come on, boy!" he called and set off in the direction of Hadley.

The puppy frisked and frolicked, running on in front of him, running back to him, leaping up at him. . . . William fixed his mind on the pleasant picture of his mother's joy and surprise on receiving fifty pounds instead of the expected one . . . but the small cold doubt at his heart grew larger and colder. . . . An Abyssinian Retriever. . . .

He entered Emmett's boldly, the puppy still frisking and frolicking at his heels.

Emmett—a stout bull-like man—was standing in the middle of the shop in check cap and shirt-sleeves, chewing a straw. William was dismayed to notice that his eyes rested on the Abyssinian Retriever with complete indifference. Perhaps he was thinking of something else and hadn't really seen it. He went nearer, his heart beating quickly.

"Please, I've brought Honest Jim's Abyssinian Retriever," he said.

Mr. Emmett spat the straw out of his mouth and stared at him.

"You've brought whose what?" he said.

"Honest Jim's Abyssinian Retriever," repeated William, the doubt now so cold and large that it sent an icy chill into every part of him. "You said you'd give fifty pounds for it."

"*Me?* Fifty *pounds*? For *that*?" exploded Mr. Emmett.

"It—it's an Abyssinian Retriever," faltered William.

"Abyssinian——? There ain't no such a breed," said Mr. Emmett indignantly.

"Well, what sort of a dog is it, then?" said William. The dog fancier inspected the claimant with undisguised contempt.

"There's hardly any sort of dog it ain't," he said at last. "Out-an'-out little mongrel, it is."

"B-but you know Honest Jim? He said——"

"Never heard of him, whoever he is. Look here, you little blighter, you're not tryin' to be funny, are you? 'Cause, if you are——"

"No," said William. "I'm not. Listen. This man, called Honest Jim, he said you knew him an' he said you'd offered him fifty pounds for this Abyss—this dog. He said——"

"I've no time for fairy tales this morning," interrupted the dog fancier impatiently. "Clear out an' take your encyclopædia with you."

"But listen," pleaded William. "Do listen. This man said——"

"Clear out!" shouted the dog fancier and, bearing down upon William and his protégé, swept them before him into the street.

There William stood for a few moments, overcome by the sheer horror of the situation. Something must be done at once—and suddenly he knew what must be done. He must get into touch with Honest Jim, return the Abyssinian Retriever to him and make him give him back his pound. He had last seen him setting off in the direction of Marleigh, so in the direction of Marleigh sped William, the puppy leaping delightedly by his side, obviously under the delusion that the whole procedure was devised for his entertainment and quite unperturbed by the slur cast on his ancestry.

There was no trace of Honest Jim in Marleigh, but a farm labourer, questioned, said that he had seen a ragged tramp with a black beard on the road to Upper Marleigh. Panting, breathless, his heart a wild confusion of hope and despair, William ran on to Upper Marleigh. . . . And there, sitting on the bench outside the Green Dragon, a mug of beer at his lips, was Honest Jim. . . . Honest Jim looked for a moment a trifle disconcerted to see William and the Abyssinian Retriever approaching him. He had intended to be far enough away by the time William realised his "mistake", but had not been able to resist the temptation to relieve a perennial thirst by means of the newly-acquired wealth . . . and time had somehow slipped by as he did so.

"I say," panted William, coming up to him, "you know this dog you sold me——"

Honest Jim put down the mug and looked at him in surprise.

"Me?" he said. "I never sold you no dawg, young sir. Never set eyes on you till this 'ere moment."

William stared at him, hardly able to believe his ears.

"B-b-but you *did*," he persisted. "You said it was an Abyssinian Retriever, an' I gave you a pound for it an'——"

"Not me, young sir," said the tramp, draining his mug. "Never set eyes on you or the dawg before," He rose. "Well, I'd better be gettin' on. . . ."

"But you *did*," said William desperately. He was on the verge of tears—a rare occurrence with William.

"I can't go back to my mother without that money. It wasn't mine or hers. It was the Poors'. I gave it you for the dog 'cause you said it was an——"

A thoughtful look had come into the tramp's face.

"Look here," he said, "did this man that sold you the dawg say his name was Honest Jim?"

"Yes," said William.

"And was he the spit'n' image of me to look at?"

"Yes," said William.

The tramp shook his head slowly and sadly.

"I know 'im, then. Me twin brother, 'e is. An' a greater scoundrel never walked this 'ere earth. 'E's done you down proper, young sir. Took your quid for a dawg that's not worth a tanner. Oh, if only I could get me 'ands on 'im! Mind you, you're not the only one 'e's done down. 'E's ruined me. If it 'adn't been for 'im I'd be ridin' in me own car this very second. Paid 'is debts over an' over again, I 'ave, to keep 'im out of prison for our poor ole mother's sake. *Ruined* meself for 'im."

William's gaze travelled doubtfully over the ragged unsavoury figure.

"He—he was dressed same as you," he said.

"That's 'is cunnin'," said the tramp with a sigh. "'E knows I'm trusted an' respected through the length an' breadth of the land, so 'e dresses same as me an' o' course 'e looks same as me to start with, so—well, you can see for yourself 'ow it is. 'E's even took me name—Honest Jim. 'E knows 'e's only to say 'e's Honest Jim an' people'll trust 'im with anythin', thinkin' it's me. Now, look 'ere, young sir"—he got up and put his mug on the seat beside him—"I'll not rest till I've got that quid back for you. I know 'is

WILLIAM'S GAZE TRAVELLED DOUBTFULLY OVER THE
RAGGED UNSAVOURY FIGURE.

'aunts an' I'll track 'im down an' get that quid o' yours
back for you if it takes me the rest of me nat'ral life.
That's me. Honest Jim. Can't rest till I've put
wrong right. That's 'ow I spends my life, tryin' to
put right wot 'e's done wrong, an' wipe the slur off me
good name. No, don't thank me till I've done it, but
—well, good-bye, young sir, an' wish me luck."

William opened his mouth to speak, but Honest
Jim was already making good his escape, moving with
surprising agility along the high road and, once out of
sight, slipping down byways and unfrequented paths
in order to put as much ground as he could between
him and possible retribution.

William sat on the bench, chin on hands, staring
gloomily into the distance. He was a credulous boy
and one who was always ready to believe the best of
his fellow creatures, but he had little doubt that
Honest Jim and his twin brother were the same. It
was a depressing thought, but still more depressing
was the thought of returning to his mother without
her eight half-crowns. The only bright spot in the
whole situation was the Abyssinian Retriever, who
sat by his feet thumping the ground at intervals
with his stubby tail and grinning contentedly at the
world around him . . . and even he was not a very
bright spot. He was the cause of the whole trouble
and must somehow be disposed of, for even the optimistic William realised that, especially in the present
circumstances, he would meet with but a cold reception
at his mother's hands.

He tried to rehearse the forthcoming scene with his
mother and to prepare his explanations and excuses.
"Yes, I got the half-crowns all right, but I bought a

dog with them. . . ." "Well, you see, this man told me that it was an Abyssinian Retriever an' . . ." No, it was no use. He couldn't make it sound convincing even to himself. He had not only let his mother down. He had robbed the poor and needy of eight half-crowns. . . . It was like a nightmare. . . . The church clock struck twelve. . . . He couldn't sit here any longer. He must go home and face his mother's anger and disappointment. . . . Then a sudden idea struck him. He could at least try to make up something of the money. He could go round begging for the Society. Someone might give him something. . . . He might perhaps get as much as one half-crown, which would be better than none. He didn't really feel very optimistic, but at least he could try. He sprang up from the bench and summoned his companion, who was nosing in a neighbouring hedge.

"Come on, boy."

The puppy, still blissfully unconscious of the trouble he had caused, frisked gaily down the road with William.

William's freckled face wore an anxious expression, and his lips moved silently as he practised his appeal. "Please could you give me a penny or two for rebuildin' the slums?" . . . "Please could you give me some money to get soup an' coal an' stuff for the poor?"

He hadn't any great hopes as, with set fierce expression, he knocked at the door of the first house he came to and began: "Please could you spare me a penny for——" but he wasn't prepared for the indignation of the housemaid, who said:

"You saucy little rascal, you!" and slammed the door in his face.

He went on to the next house. This time the mistress of the house herself answered the door. She heard him in silence, then said sadly:

"You know, little boy, that this is a very serious thing. If I chose to inform the police that you were begging like this you'd get into trouble. Now go home and play with your nice toys and never do a thing like this again."

Despite this discouragement he made a third attempt, but this time an irascible old man opened the door a few inches, shouted: "No, I can't tell you the time," and shut it with a bang before William could correct the mistake.

Slowly he wandered on down the road. He felt too much dispirited to try again, yet he could not face the prospect of returning to his mother with his story of failure.

He sat down on a stile by the roadside to consider the situation, fixing his eyes absently on a house halfway up the hill. Then gradually he began to notice the house. It was a large house. Even from the distance and seen between the trees, it wore an air of prosperity. Surely the people who lived in it could spare him half a crown. He felt that even one halfcrown might divert something of his mother's anger. It would be better, anyway, than returning emptyhanded. . . . He must try to make his plea more moving. He must manage to get it out before they could stop or misunderstand him. . . . He must make a bold bid for half a crown. . . . "Please could you give me half a crown for givin' soup to the slums . . . No, I mean givin' soup to the poor and rebuildin' the slums."

He set off up the hill, in at the big iron gates, and up a large shady drive. . . . "Please could you spare me

half a crown for soup an' coal an' rebuildin' the slums.
. . ." The puppy still frisked at his heels.

A little woman with greyish hair opened the door.

"OH, YOU'VE BROUGHT HIM!" SAID THE WOMAN
BREATHLESSLY.

"Please could you spare——" began William, but
she interrupted him, clasping her hands eagerly, her
eyes fixed on the frisking puppy.

"Oh, you've brought him!" she said breathlessly. "Oh, I am so glad. And how quick you've been! I only put the notice up half an hour ago. Oh dear, what a relief! Do come in." She snatched the puppy up and kissed it ecstatically. "Oh, Tinker, you naughty boy!"

The puppy greeted her with the exuberant delight and affection that it seemed able to extend to the whole world. Bewildered, William followed her into a small sitting-room.

"It's my little niece's dog," explained the lady. "She's staying with me for the war and she's been very ill indeed, and was getting up to-day for the first time. We haven't let the dog go into her bedroom and she's been *living* for the moment when she could play with him again, and this morning I found that he'd disappeared and I didn't know *what* to do. I knew that the child would be *heartbroken* and that it would probably send her temperature *right* up again, and I was in *despair*—especially when I heard that he'd been seen following a tramp. Then I suddenly thought of putting up that notice in the post office. Of course, I know a pound seems a large reward for a little dog like this, but it was worth it to me to get him back. I'm sure that if my little niece had come down this afternoon to find him gone, she'd never have got over it. Oh dear, oh dear! I was so dreading breaking the news to her that I was beginning to feel quite ill myself. . . . Where did you find him?"

William considered. It was a long story and there seemed no point in telling it.

"Jus' on the road," he said.

"Well, I'm so grateful to you." She took a bag

from the table and drew out a pound note. "And here's the reward. I simply won't let the little rascal out of my sight for the rest of the day."

William stared, blinked, gulped, and swallowed. The nightmare had suddenly turned into a dream. He couldn't believe it. He felt dazed and shaken, only sufficiently in command of his forces to say: "Thanks *awfully*. C-could you let me have eight half-crowns instead of the note?"

"Certainly, you funny little boy!" said the lady gaily. "I suppose it *seems* more to you that way, doesn't it? I know that my little niece would always rather have six pennies than a sixpenny piece!" She burrowed in her bag and brought out eight half-crowns. "*There* you are, and I'm *most* grateful."

"So'm I to you," said William fervently as he pocketed the coins, "an' I'd better be goin' now. It's nearly lunch-time. Good-bye an'—an' thanks *awfully*."

"Good-bye," said the lady. She stood at the front door holding the puppy in her arms. The puppy was frantically licking her face, and had obviously already forgotten both William and Honest Jim.

William walked down the road again. So great was his relief that his usually stalwart knees trembled beneath him.

"Gosh!" he ejaculated to the surrounding landscape and added still more emphatically: "*Gosh!*"

* * * * *

Mrs. Brown was awaiting him anxiously.

"Oh, there you are, William," she said. "How did you get on?"

"Oh, I got on all right," said William carelessly,

laying the eight half-crowns in a neat pile on the table. "I told you I would."

"I know," said Mrs. Brown, "but somehow I never thought you would. . . . Well, I'm very grateful to you, dear. You've been a long time, though. Did some of them keep you waiting?"

"No," said William. He thought over the events of the morning and realised that they were best consigned to oblivion. "No . . . I jus' went for a little walk round after I'd got 'em."

CHAPTER IX

A PRESENT FOR A LITTLE GIRL

WILLIAM wouldn't have noticed the little girl at all if she hadn't looked so sad. She stood at the gate of Honeysuckle Cottage, gazing into the distance with mournful tear-filled eyes. Mrs. Fountain and Miss Griffin, the former occupants of the cottage, had removed to London, and the little girl, with her mother and aunt and a baby brother, had moved in. William had heard vaguely that their name was Paget, but he was not interested in them. He regarded with complete indifference the shifting population of evacuees who occupied from time to time such cottages as fell vacant in the neighbourhood. As Mr. Moss, of the general shop, put it: "'Ere to-day an' gorn to-morrer, so wot's the use of wearin' oneself out over 'em?"

But, as he walked on towards the village, William found his thoughts dwelling on the little girl. Had she been crying or not? Certainly she had been nearly crying. . . . Beneath William's rugged exterior was a deeply hidden vein of chivalry. He didn't like to think of the little girl's being unhappy. He couldn't get it out of his head. It worried him. . . . He didn't want to, but he felt he must go back to see if she really was crying, and, in that case, to find out if he could help.

Slowly, reluctantly, he retraced his steps to Honey-suckle Cottage. The little girl still stood gazing into the distance with mournful tear-filled eyes. As William watched, a tear brimmed over and trickled down her cheek.

"What's the matter?" said William gruffly.

She looked at him.

"They're going to kill Ernest," she said, and another tear brimmed over.

"Gosh!" said William. "Is that your baby brother?"

"Goodness, no!" said the little girl, forgetting to cry for the moment. "Goodness, I wouldn't mind them killing *him*. He's a frightful nuisance. He's always pulling my things to pieces. No, Ernest's my darling little grey rabbit."

"Why are they goin' to kill him?" said William.

"They're goin' to kill him for dinner on Sunday," said the little girl. "They think he's just an ordinary rabbit, but he's *not* an ordinary rabbit. He's my darling Ernest and he knows me and wriggles his darling little nose up and down at me and—— Oh, I can't *bear* it if they kill him!" Her eyes filled with tears again. "I've told them that I won't eat any of him, and they just say I needn't. I can't bear to think of them eating Ernest. *Eating* him! Ernest!" Her voice was lost in sobs.

William watched her in sympathetic concern. He didn't think much of rabbits himself, but he could understand what she felt.

"Is he the only one?"

The little girl took out a grubby handkerchief and dried her tears.

"No. They've got *lots*. That's what's so *mean*. They've got more than twenty and yet they want to kill Ernest. Oh, it's *cruel!*" with a fresh burst of tears.

"Have you told 'em you don't want 'em to?" said William.

"'Course I have," said the little girl. "They just say it's war-time and they're only keeping rabbits for food and I must get used to eating them. They say they've left Ernest as long as they can and if they leave him any longer he won't be fit to eat."

"Where do they keep them?"

"In the back garden. Would you like to see them? You can come round. Mother and Auntie and the baby are down in Hadley, so there's no one here but me. You'll love Ernest. He's not an ordinary rabbit at all. He's got a little tuft of white hair right on the top of his head."

William followed her round to the back of the house and into a shed full of rabbit hutches. In the hutch nearest the door was a grey rabbit with a tuft of white hair on its head. The little girl opened the door of the hutch and took it into her arms.

"This is Ernest," she said, kissing it affectionately. "Isn't he sweet!"

The rabbit stared at William with an expression that could only be interpreted as a sneer.

"You *must* see him eat," said the little girl. "He's sweetest of all when he eats."

She put the rabbit back into the hutch and ran round to the vegetable garden, returning with some cabbage leaves, which she thrust through the wire netting. The rabbit ate them in the manner of his kind.

"Isn't he *lovely!*" said the little girl, clasping her

o

"ISN'T HE *LOVELY!*" SAID THE LITTLE GIRL.

hands ecstatically. "Have you ever *seen* a sweeter rabbit? Oh, dear! How can I *bear* it if they kill him?"

"Well, don't start crying again," said William.

"I can't help it," said the little girl. "I can't bear to think of it."

William was silent for a moment, then said:

"Can't you hide it?"

"How *can* I?" said the little girl. "They'd find it if I put it anywhere in my bedroom, and that's the only place I have to hide things in. I once thought of letting him go free rather than having him eaten, but I suppose, if I did, dogs or real rabbits would kill him."

She looked at William and her face suddenly shone.

"*Oh!*" she exclaimed breathlessly.

"What's the matter?" said William.

"*You* could help."

"*Me?*" said William, taken aback. "How could *I* help?"

"You could hide him for me. They'd never think of coming to your house to look for him. They'd just think he must have escaped."

"Y-yes," said William doubtfully, "but what could I *do* with him?"

"Oh, just keep him," said the little girl vaguely. "Keep him and feed him and look after him and don't let anyone know about him, of course."

"Yes, but for how long?" said William, still more doubtfully.

"Oh, till they've forgotten they were going to kill him or till he's too old to kill or till after the war."

"Yes, but *where* can I keep him?" said William.

"Anywhere," said the little girl. She spoke impatiently as if she considered that William was raising trivial and irrelevant objections. "It doesn't matter where you keep him as long as you keep him."

"Well, I don't know . . ." said William. Knight-errantry in general appealed to him but not in this particular form. He had, in any case, never met a less inspiring rabbit than Ernest. . . .

The little girl's eyes brimmed again with tears, and her lip trembled.

"I think you're being very unkind," she said. "You aren't even *trying* to help."

"I am," protested William. "Honest, I am. Listen. I'll take it. Stop cryin' an' I'll take it."

The little girl's face cleared. She smiled at him.

"Oh, *thank* you. That's lovely of you. You must take him now, 'cause they might come back an' kill him any minute and I couldn't bear it."

She opened the door of the hutch, took out Ernest and kissed him tenderly.

"Good-bye, my darling." She thrust him into William's arms. "You *will* take care of him, won't you? He likes carrots chopped up very small and warm bread and milk. And you'll see that he's warm and comfy at nights, won't you? Now take him away quickly. They'll be coming back any minute. . . ."

With obvious enjoyment of the dramatic nature of the situation, she bundled Ernest under his coat and hustled the two of them in a conspiratorial manner down to the gate.

"Don't breath a *word* to *anyone*," she said in a hoarse whisper, then closed the gate on him and ran back to the house.

William stood for a minute in the road, feeling slightly bewildered. He didn't want a rabbit. He disliked rabbits. He particularly disliked Ernest. But he'd undertaken the job and he must to see it through. He walked on slowly down the road. Ernest appeared to be of a philosophical disposition and beyond small movements of a somewhat tickling nature made no effort to escape from his confined quarters. William walked still more slowly as he approached his garden gate. He had no idea what to do with Ernest when

he got him home . . . where to keep him, how to feed
him. . . . He had read many stories of refugees secreted
in households during the Civil War and other historical crises.   It had seemed a simple enough process.
One rabbit surely could not be more difficult to con-
ceal than a Cavalier or a Roman Catholic priest.   But
William had a foreboding that Ernest would be.
He would not realise the position and would somehow
or other cause trouble.   Fortunately rabbits had not
loud voices.   Or had they?   He had never met a
bored or exasperated rabbit, and he had a suspicion
that Ernest would be both. . . .

He opened the garden gate, and there a complication
he had not foreseen met him.   For Jumble sprang upon
him in a state of wild excitement, barking furiously,
leaping up, scratching at his overcoat. . . .

"Down, Jumble!" said William, but that only
seemed to excite him the more.

Mrs. Brown came into the hall as he entered.

"What on earth's the matter with that dog?" she
said.

"Dunno," muttered William, hurrying past her to
the stairs.

Fortunately Mrs. Brown was too much taken up by
Jumble to notice the bulge under William's coat.

"I've never seen him like this before," she said.
"I believe he's going mad."

"No, he's not," said William, plunging upstairs.
"He's all right."

Jumble accompanied him, always on the stair just
in front of him, leaping up at the bulge in his overcoat,
barking furiously, growling, snarling. . . .

"Be careful, dear," said Mrs. Brown anxiously.   "He

seems to be turning quite savage. Perhaps I'd better ring up the vet."

William dived into his bedroom, slamming the door upon Jumble, who hurled himself upon it in a state of uncontrollable agitation.

In his bedroom, William brought out Ernest and put him on the bed. Ernest looked round him superciliously then sat up and scratched his ear. Jumble had thrust his nose right under the door and was snarling so violently that he could hardly get his breath.

"Jumble!" called Mrs. Brown from the hall. "William, we must do something about that dog. He's dangerous. . . ."

Jumble replied by a fresh outburst of snarls and barks. William realised that the situation must be dealt with at once. He took up Ernest, bundled him into a drawer, closed the drawer and ran downstairs, calling Jumble as he went. Jumble was loth to leave the door of William's bedroom. He sniffed and snarled for a few more moments, then turned unwillingly to obey the summons.

Mrs. Brown was standing in the hall.

"I don't like it at all, William," she said. "I've never seen him like this before."

"He's all right now," said William. "I think he was jus' a bit excited at seeing me."

"Well, if he gets any worse," said Mrs. Brown, "you'd better call in at the vet's. It doesn't look to me like ordinary excitement."

"Come on, Jumble!" said William, for Jumble had stopped at the foot of the stairs and was obviously considering a return to the scene of his recent investigations. "Come *on!*"

Reluctantly Jumble allowed himself to be dragged out of the house, down the lane, across the field and into the woods. There the multiplicity of scents drove Ernest's from his memory, and he burrowed frantically into rabbit holes and darted off after bigger and better smells till William (as he had meant to) completely lost him.

Slowly and thoughtfully William returned home.

WILLIAM STOOD AT THE GATE WATCHING GENERAL MOULT.

The situation would be simpler now that he had tem-
porarily disposed of Jumble, but even so it was far
from simple. He could not leave Ernest indefinitely
among his underclothing. He had nothing to feed him
on and didn't see the prospect of getting anything. It
was all very well for the little girl to talk glibly of
carrots chopped up small and warm bread and milk,
but where was one to obtain such things in a war-time
household? The gardener kept an eagle eye on his
vegetables and his mother on larder and store cupboard, so that Ernest, if he depended on those sources
of supply, was likely to fare badly.

As he passed General Moult's house he stopped. The
garage door was open and inside the garage could be
seen rows upon rows of rabbit hutches, each with its
occupant or occupants. He remembered that General
Moult, like most of the inhabitants of the village, had
lately "gone in for" rabbits. He had, moreover, gone
in for them very thoroughly. He had sixty or seventy,
and he spent most of the day tending and grooming
and feeding them.

He was there now, pottering about among them,
with bits of cabbage leaves and carrot-tops dangling
out of his pockets. William stood at the gate watching
him. One rabbit more or less among so many would
surely never be noticed. It would be tended and
groomed and fed along with the others. But he noticed
that all the hutches were padlocked. General Moult
was an irritable, cantankerous old gentleman with a
deep distrust of his fellow men. He had, however, like
most people, his weak spot, and William knew what it
was. The Boer War had been the high light of the
General's life, and he had taken part in the Relief of

Mafeking. Both the war of 1914 and the war of 1939 were to him petty skirmishes in comparison. When people began to talk of the Battle of the Somme or the Evacuation of Dunkirk, he tried to bring the conversation round to the Relief of Mafeking . . . and it wasn't easy. His life, in fact, was one of perpetual frustration. No one seemed to be interested any longer in the Relief of Mafeking. He couldn't understand it. . . .

William set off home at a run, eager to carry out his new plan. He was aware, of course, that it was not ideal—it afforded too many loopholes for the unexpected—but it was the best he could manage at the moment.

He opened the drawer slowly and carefully. Yes, Ernest was still there, and William noticed with some dismay that his sojourn had not improved the state of his underclothing. Ernest, on being restored to a fuller view of life, stared around him with his usual expression of supercilious disdain and scratched his ear. . . . William took him up, bundled him under his coat and hurried down the road again to General Moult's. The Mafeking veteran was still pottering about among his rabbit hutches. William approached him—warily, for he knew he was no favourite with the warrior. The General looked up as he approached.

"Now then, now then, now then!" he said testily. "What d'you want? What d'you want? Go away, boy. I'm busy."

William assumed the expression of an earnest seeker after knowledge.

"Please," he said, "I heard someone talkin' the other day an' they said you'd been at the Relief of Mafeking."

"PUT IT BACK WITH THE OTHERS," SAID THE GENERAL
IMPATIENTLY.

The testiness vanished from the General's face, and a
look of modest—almost coy—pride took its place.

"I was, my boy, I was. You were informed correctly.
I was very much at the Relief of Mafeking. Though
few people now seem to realise it, it was one of the
greatest and most important military exploits in the
history of the world."

"Yes, I think it was, too," said William. "I'm jolly

well sure it was.   I've always wanted to know 'zactly
what happened."

"Come in, come in, come in," said the General
genially.   (He had misjudged this boy, looking on him
as an incorrigible young hooligan when actually he
had a sense of historical proportion lacking in many of
his elders.)   "Come in, my boy.   Now what is it you
want to know?"

"I'd like to know everything," said William earnestly.
"Right from the beginning."

The General straightened his drooping shoulders and
twirled his drooping moustache.

"You shall, my boy," he said.   "You shall indeed.
It's all as fresh in my memory as if it had happened
yesterday. . . .   Our journey to Mafeking itself, of
course, was one of considerable difficulty.   We started
from Beira, transferred by narrow-gauge railway to
Bamboo Creek, changed to a broader gauge to Maren-
dellas, travelled in coaches to Bulawayo, after that the
five-hundred-mile journey to Ootsi.   Then began our
march of a hundred miles over some of the most
difficult country in the world.   We marched twenty-
five miles a day.   I remember one day . . ."

In his excitement he had left the door of one of the
hutches open and William murmuring: "'Scuse me.   I
think one of your rabbits has got out," darted from
the garage and dived into the bushes just outside.   He
emerged holding a grey rabbit with a white tuft on
its head.

"Put it back with the others," said the General
impatiently.   "Put it back, put it back. . . .   Well,
the two columns arrived at Masibi Stadt within an
hour of each other, to find that the enemy had

possession of the only water supply and of the hills surrounding it. . . ."

William heaved a sigh of relief. There was Ernest comfortably housed and with the prospect of a decent supper. Ernest, for his part, sat up and surveyed the other occupants of the hutch with his most offensive sneer and began to scratch himself. It was a relief, but William realised that it had to be paid for. The General, having found what he supposed to be an appreciative audience, after years of waiting, was not going to let him off lightly. It was a worn and exhausted boy, who, three-quarters of an hour later, staggered out of General Moult's front door. . . .

He found the little girl in the lane outside his own home. She wore an exaggeratedly conspiratorial air and glanced around her in the manner of a film spy, as, lowering her voice to a whisper, she said:

"Where is he? I've come to see him."

William was taken aback. Somehow he hadn't expected that visits to the evacuee would form part of the programme.

"He—he's not in at the minute," he said.

The little girl's expression registered resentful suspicion.

"Not in?" she echoed. "What d'you mean, not in? You've got him, haven't you? If—you've—gone —and—lost—him——"

Her eyes took on a glassy stare and her voice a low threatening tone. William realised that, despite her sex and size, she could be dangerous.

"No, I haven't," he said nervously. "Honest, I haven't. He's jus'—gone away for a bit. He's quite safe an' he's havin' a jolly good time. You see, my dog didn't sort of take to him, so I took him away to stay with a friend for a bit."

The little girl was scowling at him in a manner that detracted considerably from her charm.

"Where is he?" she demanded.

William realised that it would be fatal to reveal Ernest's whereabouts to her. She would haunt General Moult's garage, and trouble would inevitably ensue.

"I can't tell you that," he said, lowering his voice and copying her conspiratorial manner. "It's a secret. I can't tell you why, but it's gotter be a secret. He— he sends you his love."

For some strange reason this seemed to satisfy the little girl. Her scowl cleared and she nodded.

"You're *sure* he's all right?" she said.

"Quite sure," said William. "This friend that's looking after him for me, he's crazy on rabbits, and he thinks Ernest's the finest one he's ever seen."

The little girl sighed.

"I miss him terribly," she said. "I feel so sad and lonely without him."

"He misses you, too," said William, "but he's havin' a jolly good time all the same."

"When can I go and see him?" said the little girl.

"Well," said William, "this friend and me talked it over an' we thought it was safer for you not to go an' see him. We thought it might get round to your mother an' aunt if you did, an' they'd go and get him back an' kill him. He's pretendin' it's his own rabbit jus' to put people off the scent."

Again the little girl nodded, satisfied. She was evidently a little girl with a weakness for intrigue, and she liked to feel plots thicken around her.

For the next few days William carefully avoided both her and General Moult. The situation was, he realised, a complicated one, and complicated situations were best left to themselves.

He felt a little apprehensive when his mother said one morning: "I've asked Mrs. Paget and her little girl to lunch to-morrow. It's very lonely for them away from home, and I thought it would be a nice change for them."

"I don't think we oughter have people to lunch in war-time," said William virtuously. "I think it's wrong."

"Oh no, William," said Mrs. Brown. "We must be neighbourly."

"Neighbourly," snorted William. "To *her!* Huh!"

There was no reason why the subject of Ernest should obtrude itself on a quiet war-time luncheon party, but from the beginning William had a suspicion that it would.

At first everything went smoothly. Mrs. Paget talked volubly about the superiority of her home surroundings to those among which she now found herself, while her daughter ate her way stolidly and silently through her portion of "game pie," eyeing William occasionally in a thoughtful manner that, William felt, boded no good. He suspected that very shortly he would be put through another searching cross-examination on Ernest's whereabouts and well being. . . . He had not seen Ernest since depositing him in his new home. He had felt that he couldn't endure another description of the Relief of Mafeking, and he was afraid of rousing the General's suspicions by an undue interest in his unofficial evacuee.

They went into the garden after lunch.

"There's nothing to see but a few vegetables, of course," said Mrs. Brown, "but the carrots are going to be really good this year."

"You don't keep rabbits?" said Mrs. Paget.

"No," said Mrs. Brown. "I haven't time to look after them, and William would never remember."

"Jumble's not keen on 'em," put in William.

"One of ours escaped the other day," said Mrs.

THE LITTLE GIRL WINKED AT WILLIAM BEHIND **HER**
MOTHER'S BACK.

Paget. "I don't suppose he lived long. He wouldn't be able to feed himself in a wild state."

The little girl winked at William behind her mother's back and gave him an elaborately secret smile.

"That was a delicious game pie we had at lunch," went on Mrs. Paget.

"Oh, it was just odds and ends," smiled Mrs. Brown. "A neighbour of ours, General Moult, had kindly sent round a rabbit. We had to skin and clean it ourselves, which was rather a nuisance. I believe that they take the skins as war salvage. I must ask the dustman. There it is. I put it out to dry."

They all turned to look at the skin, which hung on a hook outside the kitchen door. It was quite an ordinary rabbit skin except that there was a tuft of white between the ears.

The secret smile dropped from the little girl's face and a look of dawning horror took its place. William's heart sank. Gosh! He'd never thought of that. He'd never thought that General Moult might kill Ernest and give him away. And to his mother of all people! Gosh! There didn't seem to be any justice in the world. . . .

"Well, shall we go indoors and sit down comfortably?" said Mrs. Brown, unaware of the bombshell she had dropped. "You children can stay out in the garden."

"I—I think I'd like to go indoors an' sit down comfortably, too," said William. "I—I think I feel a bit tired."

"Nonsense, dear!" said Mrs. Brown. "You must stay out here and look after your little guest. . . . *You'd* like to stay out in the garden, wouldn't you, dear?"

"Yes," said the little girl, fixing a grim accusing gaze on William.

"That's right," said Mrs. Brown placidly, going indoors with her guest and leaving William to his fate.

"*Now!*" said the little girl grimly, as soon as they had gone. "What's the name of that friend you said you'd left Ernest with?"

"I can't tell you," said William. "I told you I couldn't tell you. It's a secret. It's gotter be a secret."

The little girl's face was a mask of quivering fury.

"If it was General Moult and if—it—was—Ernest—we—had—in—that—pie——"

"'Course it wasn't," said William, but without much conviction. "'*Course* it wasn't."

"Then take me to him and show him me," said the little girl.

"I can't," said William desperately. "Not jus' now. I keep tellin' you. It wouldn't be safe."

With one of her swift dramatic changes of mood, the little girl abandoned her fury and burst into tears.

"I can't bear it," she sobbed. "You cruel boy to pretend to help me and then make me eat him! *Eat* him! I'd rather have *died* than eaten my darling Ernest. Oh, I can't bear it!" Her sobs increased in volume. "You cruel boy! I *hate* you!"

William glanced anxiously towards the house. Her voice had taken on a shrill hysterical note and at any moment might attract the notice of his mother or hers. Then the whole story would come out, and he, of course, would be blamed.

P

"Now look here," he said reassuringly. "It's all right. Don't you worry about it. 'Course it wasn't Ernest."

"If it wasn't Ernest, then," she said stormily, "get Ernest back for me."

"All right," he said. "All right. I'll do that all right. Now don't you cry any more."

For a moment her face cleared then she broke out into a shrill wail.

"Oh, but if you do, they'll only kill him for dinner, and I couldn't *bear* it."

"Now don't you worry," said William. "I'll fix it up for you all right. You jus' stop cryin' an' I'll fix it up."

"And I haven't eaten him, have I?" said the little girl. "If I have, I'll start crying again and I shan't *ever* be able to stop."

She was already gathering breath for a fresh burst of tears.

"'Course you haven't," said William hastily. "'*Course* you haven't."

"And you'll get him back for me? I can't go on living without him."

"Course I'll get him back for you," promised William.

"And not let them kill him for dinner when you've got him back for me?"

"'Course not," said William rather faintly as he realised the rashness of these promises.

"All right," said the little girl with the air of one conceding a great favour. "Then I won't start crying again."

At that moment Mrs. Paget came out of the house, followed by Mrs. Brown.

"We must go now, dear," she said to the little girl. "Thank William for the lovely time you've had."

"And I'm sure William's enjoyed it, too, haven't you, William?" said Mrs. Brown.

"Yes, haven't I!" said William, with a mirthless smile.

The next morning, immediately after breakfast, William went round to General Moult's. . . . General Moult was there, pottering about among his hutches. . . . William threw a quick glance around and to his immense relief saw Ernest sitting inside the wire netting nibbling a cabbage leaf. There was no mistaking him. It was certainly Ernest. Even while eating his cabbage leaf, he continued to survey his surroundings with his usual air of sneering contempt.

"Yes?" said the General, turning round as William entered. "What is it? What is it?"

"I didn't quite understand," said William, who had thought up the question on the way, "when you were telling me about the Relief of Mafeking, how the other column got there, the one you joined up with."

"Didn't I make that clear?" said the General, brightening. "Well, I think I'd better start again right at the beginning. I mean, the whole thing is such a—a whole. If you don't understand one part you don't understand any of it. Well, my boy . . ."

It took longer—much longer—than last time. The General had remembered many more details in the meantime and was delighted at having an opportunity of bringing them out. It began among the rabbit hutches and continued in the General's study, the table littered with maps and the ancient notebooks in which

"I WANT TO GIVE IT TO A LITTLE GIRL," SAID WILLIAM.

the General had kept his diaries during the campaign.
It was nearly lunch-time when William staggered out,
pale and exhausted. . . . But he had not forgotten
the object of his visit.

"Please, can I have another look at your rabbits
before I go?" he asked.

"Certainly, my boy," said the General genially.   He was once again the debonair young officer who had been such a success with Boer children.   He had a snapshot of himself giving a Boer child, about William's age, a ride on his horse.   "Certainly, my boy.   Nice little creatures, rabbits.   There were quite a lot on the veldt, I remember.   Bigger than these, of course, and with a much better flavour."

William took up his position in front of Ernest, watched him for a few minutes in silence, then heaved a long and gusty sigh.

"What's the matter, my boy?" said the General.

"I wonder if you can tell me how to get a rabbit like that," said William.

"What d'you want it for?" said the General.

"I want to give it to a little girl," said William. "She says she wants a rabbit jus' like that—with a white blob on its head—an' I'd like to give it her."

"Haw, haw!" chuckled the General.   "So that's it, is it?   A present for a little girl!   Haw, haw!   Well, take it, my boy, take it.   I sent your mother one just like it the other day.   Oddly enough, I didn't realise I'd got two of 'em just alike, but with so many, of course, one's apt to lose track. . . .   By the way, my boy, before we actually attacked Mafeking we'd been strengthened by the addition of C Battery of four twelve-pounder guns of Canadian Artillery and a small body of Queenslanders.   They'd come from Beira, making a detour of thousands of miles and arrived in the nick of time. . . ."

"Yes," said William, "yes, that's jolly int'restin' . . . About this rabbit.   You see, this little girl's mother keeps rabbits an' the other day one escaped an' she

might think this one was that one back an' kill it for
dinner. The little girl doesn't want it to be killed.
She wants it for a pet."

"Haw, haw!" chuckled the General. "I remember
we had a rabbit for a pet when we were children.
Haw, haw! Or was it a goat? 'Pon my soul, I forget.
But we had a pet. Yes, yes, I'm pretty sure we had
a pet. . . . Now about this rabbit. Tell you what,
my boy. I'll write a letter to the child's mother and
tell her that I've given the rabbit to you to give to
the little girl for the little girl to keep as a pet. That
should put the matter fair and square and above board,
shouldn't it? A present for a little girl! Bless my
soul! Haw, haw! I'll go and write it now."

He went into the house and returned a few minutes
later with an envelope which he gave to William.
Then he unlocked the door of Ernest's hutch, took him
out by the ears and put him into William's arms.

"There, my boy. That should simplify the situation
for you. A present for a little girl! Haw, haw! And
proof positive that it's not one of the run-away family
rabbits. Haw, haw! No, I've had that rabbit since
it was born. Must have done or it wouldn't be here.
Take it, my boy, with my good wishes and good luck
to you! . . . Oh, by the way, these Queenslanders I
just mentioned were part of a small army that had
come with General Carrington and . . ."

It was not till half an hour later that William
managed to escape, still clutching Ernest, and make
his way to the little girl's house.

He found her sitting on the wooden seat in the back
garden. On her knee was a large fluffy Chinchilla
rabbit.

WILLIAM FOUND HER SITTING ON A WOODEN SEAT
IN THE BACK GARDEN.

"Oh, do come and look at him, William," she called.
"Isn't he *lovely!* Auntie's brought him from Hadley for
me. They keep these for their fur so he won't ever be
killed. Isn't he *beautiful!* I'm calling him Laurence."

William brought Ernest from under his coat and
the letter from his pocket.

"I've brought Ernest back," he said, "an' here's a
note from Gen'ral Moult, sayin' that he's not to be

killed 'cause he's a present from him an' he's gotter be a pet."

The little girl stared at Ernest with an expression of contempt that almost rivalled Ernest's own.

"Oh, *that* thing!" she said. "Goodness, I'd quite forgotten it! It's only an ordinary table rabbit. Mother!" she called, "here's this ole rabbit back we lost.   Can we have it for supper?"

CHAPTER X

HUBERT'S PARTY

IT was Mrs. Monks' idea that the children whose fathers were not serving in the forces should give a party to the children whose fathers were serving in the forces. "Such a nice gesture," she said, adding vaguely: "Of course, it will take a little organising." It took more organising than she had realised, for evacuees had swollen the child population of the village to many times its pre-war figure. It was finally decided that, though all the children of men serving in the forces must attend the party, it would be impossible to find room for all the others. They, therefore, as hosts and hostesses, must provide the tea and entertainment, but only half a dozen of them must actually attend the party, and the half-dozen must be chosen by lot. Excitement rose high as the time for the drawing of the lots came near. They were drawn by Mrs. Monks herself, looking like a composite incarnation of Fate and Justice. The names were William, Ginger, a boy called Ralph, and three little girls of the type who are seen and not heard and give no trouble. There was, of course, a good deal of disappointment; but, on the whole, people were sporting about it. Even if their children were not to be at the party, they promised to give what help they could.

All except Mrs. Lane. And Mrs. Lane was furious. If darling Hubie were not to be at the party, she said, she wouldn't raise a finger to help. On the contrary, she would do all she could to hinder. It was a shame, it was a scandal, it was a conspiracy. Hubie was heart-broken. She would never forgive them for it. She went to Mrs. Monks' and made a scene. She went to Mrs. Brown's and made a scene. She went to Ginger's home and made a scene. She went to the homes of the three little girls and made scenes. She told them all that it was a shame and a scandal and a conspiracy, and that Hubert had more right than any of them to go to the party and that they wouldn't get a crumb or a penny out of her, so they needn't waste their time trying. She added that Hubert's father was just as angry as she was about it and that no one need think they were going to take an insult like this lying down, because they weren't. . . .

"A foolish woman," said Mrs. Monks, and dismissed the whole thing with an airy wave of her hand. Having launched the idea of a party, she left it to sink or swim. Mrs. Monks was always doing that, launching things and leaving them to sink or swim. She had Ideas and a mind above details, and already-overworked people were always finding themselves saddled with the organisation of Mrs. Monks' casually launched Ideas, while Mrs. Monks herself passed gaily on to fresh fields, disclaiming all further responsibility.

The responsibility in this case fell chiefly upon William's mother and Ginger's mother, Mrs. Brown and Mrs. Merridew. Ralph's mother was away, and the mothers of the three little girls said quite frankly that they could hardly find food for their own children,

MRS. LANE TOLD THEM ALL THAT IT WAS A SHAME
AND A SCANDAL AND A CONSPIRACY.

much less other people's. So Mrs. Brown and Mrs. Merridew set out upon the thankless task of obtaining provisions for the party. People were kind and did all they could, but there was little to spare from the family rations, and so small were the offers of tea and butter and jam and cake that Mrs. Brown said despairingly: "There'll hardly be a mouthful for each of them."

To make things worse, the Lanes had hit on a revenge that anyone who knew them might have foreseen. If Hubert were not to go to the village party, then Hubert should have a party of his own, and it should outshine the village party as the sun outshines the moon. It happened that the Lanes were little troubled by rationing problems. Mr. Lane had what his wife sometimes referred to as "Ways and Means," and sometimes as "Influence." Whatever this meant, the fact remained that the Lanes had meat and poultry in abundance, almost as much fat and tea and sugar (even icing sugar) as in pre-war days and tinned goods on a wholesale scale without having to consider such details as "points." It was common knowledge, of course, that Mrs. Lane had "hoarded" shamelessly from the first whisper of scarcity, but even that did not account for the flourishing state of the Lane larder. Mr. Lane generally brought a laden suit-case back with him each evening from town, and Mrs. Lane did her bit by going round every shop in Hadley every day and buying up whatever she could find in it.

With characteristic cunning, they decided to hold the party the day after the village party, in order to emphasise the comparison. If they were to hold it on the same day as the village party, everyone would be too busy to compare them, but the next day, when the news of the sparsely-provided party in the Village Hall had spread through the neighbourhood, the news of the Lane feast should burst on the world like a blaze of glory, and the children who had eaten of bread and scrape and characterless buns there could gather in the road outside the Lane house and watch through the window the Lane guests stuffing themselves on pre-war dainties.

"*That'll* teach them to leave Hubie out of things!" said Mrs. Lane viciously.

All Hubert's friends were invited and all Hubert's friends accepted the invitation.

Hubert was not an original child and could think of no other tactics than his familiar ones of shouting out to the prospective guests of the rival party the dainties that were being prepared for his own.

"Jellies and cream!" said William incredulously. "You can't *get* jellies and you can't get cream."

"My father can," sniggered Hubert.

"Your father's a black marketer," said William sternly.

Hubert smiled his sly smile.

"You can't prove it," he said, "and that's all that matters."

Mrs. Brown and Mrs. Merridew did their best. Miss Milton, after saying she could give them nothing, relented and sent round a quarter of a pound of caraway seeds. Mrs. Monks brought round a tin of powdered milk but sent for it back later the same evening because she'd "run out." General Moult offered a rabbit and a couple of cabbages, neither of which Mrs. Brown thought would be suitable. Mrs. Bott was away—unfortunately, for, though difficult of temper, she was not ungenerous. By a persistence quite alien to her nature, Mrs. Brown succeeded in "raking together," as she put it, the nucleus of a tea, but she began to look worn and haggard. The day before the party was to be held, however, William came home and found her to his surprise looking quite cheerful.

"Well, it's off," she said, "and I can't say I'm sorry."

"Off?" repeated William.

"The party. They've got mumps in the village school, so we've all agreed that it's best to put it off."

"It wouldn't have been much of one," said William gloomily. "I don't know whether it's better to have a rotten one or none at all with ole Hubert Lane havin' the sort of one he's goin' to have. It was all spoilt, anyway."

"Never mind, dear," said Mrs. Brown, "we'll try to have a really nice one later on, when," with vague optimism, "things are a bit easier. Now will you be really helpful, William, and take out these notices cancelling the party? I've got them all ready and addressed. There's one for each child who was coming to the party. You'll take them, won't you, dear?"

"Yes," said William dispiritedly. "It's a rotten ending to it all, though. Hubert Lane'll crow over us more than ever. I'd thought out some jolly good games for it, too."

William walked slowly past the Lanes' house on his way to the old barn. The party was to be held to-morrow, and Hubert's Aunt Emmy had come over to help. She stood at the gate now talking to a neighbour. William looked at her with interest. She was vague and elderly and good-natured and short-sighted and absent-minded. He chuckled as he remembered the trick that he and the Outlaws had once played on her. She did not recognise him and went on talking to the neighbour.

"Yes, Hubie and his mother have gone to London to get chocolates and sweets for the party. They know a place where they can get them. Eight-and-six a pound, mind you, but that's nothing to them. Everything else is ready—cakes, jellies, trifles, everything. I believe in having everything ready the day before, don't you? You never know what might go wrong on the day, and if you've got everything ready —well, you've got everything ready, haven't you? We've given the maid the day off to make up for the extra work to-morrow and——"

William passed on down the road, still chuckling at the memory of the trick they had once played on Aunt Emmy. That had had to do with a party of Hubert's, too. They had locked Hubert and his guests into the attic just before tea and then impersonated them at the tea table. Aunt Emmy had been officiating in Mrs. Lane's absence and had never realised that they were not the same boys who had arrived for the party earlier in the afternoon.

He had reached the main road and was just going to climb the stile by the Village Hall leading to the old barn when he noticed a little group of children standing patiently outside the door. They shone with cleanliness. They wore obviously their best clothes. Their faces glowed with eager expectation. William approached them. There was an uneasy feeling at the pit of his stomach.

"What are you waiting for?" he asked.

They turned their glowing faces to him.

"We're waiting for the doors to open for the party," they said simply.

The uneasy feeling at the pit of William's stomach

THESE CHILDREN HAD COME TO A PARTY THAT DIDN'T EXIST.

increased in intensity. He remembered the little pile of notices that his mother had given him to distribute, remembered taking them upstairs, meaning to distribute them when he went out with Ginger later in the evening, remembered going out to meet Ginger at the old barn. He hadn't taken the notices with him. He hadn't distributed them. He hadn't in fact given them another thought from the moment his mother had handed them to him till now. They were still in the drawer in his dressing-table into which he had carelessly slipped them on going upstairs, because there didn't seem to be room for them anywhere else. These children had come to a party that didn't exist . . . and it was all his fault. He opened his mouth to explain, then closed it again, staring at them in silent horror. He didn't know how to tell them. A little boy and girl joined the group. The little girl wore a pink silk dress that reached her ankles, and the little boy a velveteen suit. William realised that the garments were wildly unsuitable, but he realised, too, that it would be tragic for them, having put them on, just to go home and take them off again. He felt like Cain, like Nero, like Hitler himself, like all the villains he had ever heard of.

"There—there isn't a party," he managed to say at last.

"Yes, there is," said the little girl in the pink silk dress confidently. "We've had invitations to it."

"And it's after the time," said another little girl. "It's time they opened the doors."

A little boy put his ear to the keyhole.

"I think I can hear them," he said with a happy smile.

Ω

It was plain that he pictured frantic last-minute preparations behind the closed doors—gay decorations, laden tables, bustling aproned "helpers." His eyes were almost popping out of his face with excitement. And, behind the closed doors, as William alone of the group knew, was a bare, empty room, the forms piled up, the trestle tables stacked against the wall. . . . More children were joining the group every minute.

"I tell you there isn't any——" began William hoarsely, then stopped.

He was going to say again that there wasn't any party, but suddenly he realised that there was a party. There was a party, ready and complete, only a few yards away. There was Hubert Lane's party. . . . The guests were gazing at him in silence, waiting for him to finish his sentence. Some still looked eager and confident, but in the eyes of others there was a dawning horror, as if half expecting some incredible and crushing blow. There *couldn't* be no party, after all. There *couldn't* . . . William formed his plans swiftly. Aunt Emmy was still Aunt Emmy. A trick that had succeeded once sometimes succeeded again. No harm in trying, anyway. . . .

"The party's not being here," he said. "It's been changed. It's at another place. I'll take you to it."

A buzz of eager comment arose and they swarmed trustingly around him.

"Where is it?" "Come on!" "Let's go there quick!" "Is it far?"

Like the Pied Piper of Hamelin, William set off down the road, followed by the festive train of excited chattering children. Down the road . . . in at the green painted gate of the Lanes' house. William knocked at the door with quickly beating heart. Suppose that Hubert and his mother had already returned. Generally, when they went to London, they came home by a late train, partly to show their superiority to people who bought "cheap day tickets," and so had to come home early, partly in order that Hubert might see some film that was likely to come to Hadley later, so that, when it did come, he could say: "*That* old thing! Good Lord! I saw it in London *ages* ago!" But to-day, as the party had been arranged for to-morrow, they might come back earlier, might come back any minute, might be back already . . . Aunt Emmy opened the door, and William drew a quick breath of relief. The house seemed empty and silent. There were no signs of the return of Hubert and his mother. Aunt Emmy gazed in surprise and bewilderment at the crowd of children that filled the front garden.

"Please, we've come to the party," said William, assuming a bland expression.

Aunt Emmy's surprise and bewilderment gave place to consternation.

"B-b-but the party's not till to-morrow," she stammered.

"No, it's to-day," said William firmly. He turned to his flock. "It's to-day, isn't it?"

A shrill chorus arose.

"Yes, it *is* to-day." "Yes, it *said* to-day." "It *said* to-day on the card." "It *said* it."

"To-day . . ." "To-day . . ." "To-day . . ." they clamoured anxiously.

Aunt Emmy had grown pale.

"There must have been some mistake. I suppose

"I'M 'FRAID WE CAN'T COME TO-MORROW," SAID
WILLIAM.

they put the wrong date on the card. Oh, dear, oh
dear, what *shall* I do? . . . Listen, children, there's been
a mistake. Can you all come back to-morrow at the
same time?"

"No," said William politely but firmly, "I'm 'fraid
we can't come to-morrow." He turned to his followers: "We can't come to-morrow, can we?"

"No," shrilled his followers anxiously. To-morrow?
To-morrow didn't exist. Only to-day and to-day's

party existed. To-morrow? There was no such
thing. . . .

Still politely but very firmly, William pushed past
Aunt Emmy into the hall. His flock swarmed after
him.

"Shall we take our things off here?" he asked, and
without waiting for an answer announced: "We'll take
our things off here."

Coats, hats, scarves were flung on to hatstand, chest,
and floor, then, eagerly expectant, the flock swarmed
into the drawing-room in the wake of its self-appointed
leader.

Aunt Emmy stood in a sea of coats and hats and
scarves, staring wildly around her. It was like a
nightmare. What should she do? Oh dear, oh dear,
oh dear, what *should* she do? Then the nice polite
little boy who had been at the head of the children
came out of the drawing-room and said politely:
"Shall I help you get tea while the others play games
in there?"

It seemed to Aunt Emmy what she always called
a *lead*. She'd never been able to do anything without
a *lead*. She had to be *shown* what to do and then she
could do it. She couldn't do anything otherwise.
She was that sort of person. And this nice helpful
little boy seemed to be *showing* her, to be giving her a
lead. Now that the party was actually here, the only
thing to do, of course, was to give it the tea that had
been prepared for it. After all, if it couldn't come to-
morrow, it stood to reason that it must have it to-day.
She knew that Hubert and his mother had an engagement for the day after to-morrow, and things didn't keep
indefinitely . . . She hoped that Hubert and his mother

would think she had done the right thing.   Anyway,
she couldn't turn dear Hubert's little guests from the
door when the party tea was actually there ready for
them. . . .   What a good thing she'd got everything
ready the day before!   It always paid to be prepared.
The nice helpful little boy was already carrying trifles,
jellies, cakes, biscuits from the larder to the dining-
room. . . .   So kind of him!   The maid's being out
made things a little difficult, of course, but one must
just do the best one could. . . .

"It won't take me a minute to set the table," she
said.   "Then I'll make some bread and butter.
Everything's ready but that."

"Don't you bother with bread and butter," said the
little boy.   "No one'll eat it with all this."

"There's just the lemonade and tea, then," said
Aunt Emmy.   "Oh dear!   Hubert *will* be sorry to
have missed you."

"I bet he will," said the little boy.

"You must all make yourselves at home till he
comes and he might come any minute.   It *would* be
nice if he came now before we started tea, wouldn't it?"

"Wouldn't it!" agreed the little boy.

"I think I'm doing the right thing, don't you?" said
Aunt Emmy anxiously.

The little boy assured her that she was.

Meantime, the party in the drawing-room was
certainly "making itself at home."   Shouts of laughter,
bumps, bangs issued from the room.

"I'm sure that, even though Hubert isn't here,"
said Aunt Emmy, "he'll be glad to hear that they
enjoyed it."

"Won't he just!" said the little boy.

WILLIAM DIDN'T KNOW QUITE WHAT HE WAS GOING
TO DO IF HUBERT AND HIS MOTHER APPEARED.

"Well, I think everything's ready now," said Aunt
Emmy. "Here's a box of crackers that Hubert's
father had a great deal of difficulty in getting. We
mustn't forget those!"

"Rather not!" agreed the little boy.

"And now, dear, will you call them in to tea?"

William called them in to tea. They swarmed
across the hall into the dining-room, then stood, trans-
fixed by amazement, gazing at the jellies, trifles, jugs of
cream, iced cake, chocolate biscuits . . . Few of them
had ever seen such a feast in their lives. None of them
had seen it since the war started.

"I'm so sorry there's been this mistake," said Aunt Emmy, "but you must all try and imagine dear Hubie here, going about among his little guests, so happy to see you all enjoying yourselves. And now eat everything up. That's what Hubie would want you to do."

"Wouldn't he just!" said the little boy.

William took his own seat by the window, so that he could keep an eye on the gate. He didn't know quite what he was going to do if Hubert and his mother appeared . . . but his immediate aim was to get the tea eaten up as quickly as possible. He did his own share towards accomplishing this, and encouraged the others to do theirs, though, indeed, little encouragement was needed. Aunt Emmy fluttered about, serving jelly and trifle, cutting cake, refilling cups and saying at intervals: "I'm sure I've done the right thing. It was the only thing I could do. Now try to enjoy yourselves as much as if Hubie were here, children."

The children certainly enjoyed themselves. Urged on by William, they soon cleared up everything, leaving empty jelly dishes, empty trifle dishes, empty cake and biscuit plates, empty jugs of cream. Then they pulled the crackers and the air resounded with shrieks of laughter and the blowing of musical instruments.

"And now what would you like to do?" said Aunt Emmy when comparative quiet was restored.

"We'll have some games, shall we?" suggested William.

"Yes, dear," said Aunt Emmy, "if you know some nice quiet ones."

It appeared that William knew plenty of games, though perhaps the description "quiet" did not apply to any of them. Fortunately Aunt Emmy was rather deaf, and was busy washing up in the kitchen. It was a good thing, she thought, as she plunged the empty dishes into the water, that she had that nice helpful little boy to entertain the guests. Hubert *would* be grateful to him. . . .

Meantime, the party rampaged up and down stairs, shouted and romped and scuffled and played those "rough" games that children always tend to play when there is no grown-up at hand to quell them.

Suddenly, when the party was a seething struggling mass of attackers and defenders half-way up the staircase, the telephone bell rang, and Aunt Emmy went from the kitchen to answer it. William listened anxiously.

"Yes, dear," he heard Aunt Emmy say. "Yes, dear . . . No, dear . . . Oh, one moment, dear——" Then she put down the receiver.

"That was Hubert's mother, dear," she said to William. "They're at the station and coming along at once. She rang up to tell me I needn't do anything about supper because they're bringing something, but she rang off before I'd time to tell her about the party. . . . Still, they'll be here in a few minutes now, so you won't miss them, after all. I'm so glad."

But it appeared that William would miss them. He couldn't wait. He had to go that very second. And, oddly enough, so had all the other guests. They found themselves hustled into hats and coats and chivied out of the house by William before they could get their breath.

"B-b-b-but won't you just stay and see Hubert?" said the bewildered Aunt Emmy.

It appeared that none of them could.

"So sorry," said William. "Thanks awfully for a

"CAME TO-DAY!" ECHOED MRS. LANE. "WHAT ON
EARTH DO YOU MEAN?"

lovely party," and vanished into the dusk, sweeping his flock before him.

Chattering excitedly, discussing the tea they had eaten and the games they had played, they swarmed down the lane. At the bend in the lane they ran into two shadowy figures, laden with parcels. These stopped and stared in amazement at the crowd of youthful revellers. The last youthful reveller stopped in his turn and spoke through the dusk.

"Thanks awfully for the party, Hubert," he said.

Mrs. Lane burst into the house, followed by the laden Hubert.

"What on earth's happened?" she said, gazing at the chaos around her.

"It's the party," said Aunt Emmy. "I haven't had time to clear up yet. They've only just gone."

"Who've only just gone?" demanded Mrs. Lane.

"The party. You put the wrong date on. They came to-day."

"Came *to-day!*" echoed Mrs. Lane. "What on earth do you mean?"

"I keep telling you, dear," said Aunt Emmy patiently. "The party came to-day. You put the wrong date on the invitation cards."

"I'm quite sure I did no such thing," said Mrs. Lane.

"You must have done, dear," persisted Aunt Emmy, "because they came to-day and, as they said they couldn't come to-morrow, I let them stay. It seemed the only thing to do. They said they'd enjoyed it just as much as if Hubert had been here, and they certainly seemed to enjoy it. One of them was such a nice, helpful little boy. He said his name was William Brown."

Hubert's howl of rage and desolation rent the peaceful evening air.

William, who had crept back to listen, set off homeward, satisfied. He was going home, he knew, to Retribution, but the memory of that howl of Hubert's would be ample compensation for whatever lay in store for him.

THE END